K'ing Kung Fu #7:

Mark of the Vulture

Marshall Macao

K'ING KUNG FU #7: MARK OF THE VULTURE

MARSHALL MACAO

COPYRIGHT 2007 SILK PAGODA

PUBLISHED BY ARRANGEMENT WITH THE OLYMPIA PRESS.

ISBN: 1-59654-408-2

SILK PAGODA IS AN IMPRINT OF

DISRUPTIVE PUBLISHING.

PROLOGUE

"Master replaces Master in the bodily cycle of living and dying: and in your time, Chong Fei K'ing, Son of the Flying Tiger, you will be first among the Masters. My enemies will not be yours: for mine are dead. Yet there is but one enemy, with an infinity of faces. And all my fights, you must fight again."

—Lin Fong

SOUTH DAKOTA, THE BLACK HELLS, 1898. The young man had travelled far to sit on these heavy horse blankets and to press the stem of the ceremonial pipe between his lips. His Master had told him that Dire Wolf would soon die, and that this honored medicine man of the once mighty Sioux nation was a man worth listening to. So the young man had weathered streams and mountains and the hundred small indignities that were the lot of a Chinaman in the Western United States these days, and had come to see whether or not the bleak, beautiful mountains of the American West could teach him anything that the rolling golden plains of his native land had not.

He had not been disappointed. Dire Wolfs wisdom had, in the few days he had been here, enveloped him like a soothing mist, and he had come to understand why his Master had said of the old Indian that he was more like a tree than a man. The young man had enjoyed this week beyond anything his Master had hinted at: it had been, indeed, like resting beneath the branches of a great shade tree. Sitting here now, in the smoke-thick tipi that was home to Dire Wolf and the few remaining members of his once large family, the young man for the first time in months felt the weight of an immense burden lifted from his shoulders.

He was not sure whether that burden was the gnawing sense of incompletion he felt because he had not yet found his arch enemy Yang Tan, or whether it was the awesome responsibility which had been laid on his youthful shoulders at having been made, recently, the youngest Master of the Earthly Center in the long history of the Blue Circle. Whatever it was, the burden was lighter here.

Here, in these isolated mountains, he had relaxed and listened with undisguised pleasure as the old Indian told him stories of the bright days of his own youth. Tales of the days before the

3

white man was master in this land—the days when buffalo had filled the prairies and the fish were so thick they could be taken by hand.

But now his friend was troubled. His resonant old voice seemed close to cracking with the admission of an unaccustomed weakness.

For tonight was the night of the Autumn Equinox. At each-of the fires of the small encampment, at each of the trading posts within the small reservation which the United States Government had allotted to this proud and defeated people, the men were telling tales of the coming of the creature they called the Deathbird. Dire Wolf's brow was furrowed and he shook his head sadly.

"Lin," he said, "I do not know now whose medicine is greater. These are the bad years for the Indian, and in these years the power of Evil is often as great as the power of Good.

"When I was young, when the hills had game enough for all, before the Custers and the Keoghs came... in those days I was sure of my medicine, and I had no fear of the Deathbird. But tonight I do not know. The days are hard, and sometimes an old man needs help from younger men."

His face was dark with worry, but his eyes were soft, and Lin Fong nodded respectfully at the reference to his youth, as if to promise the aging shaman any help he had to offer. The elder smiled and continued.

"Tonight is the Night of the Crying Moon. In the old days it meant the beginning of the harvest season, but now that we are dependent on the good wishes of men in Washington for our food, it has lost this meaning and taken on another meaning. Each year on this day, the young men of our tribe paint themselves as in the old days. They dance all night long and they call to the old gods and they curse the white man in the old, old tongue of our people. They think that this makes them mighty warriors again."

Dire Wolf paused as Lin passed the long smoking pipe to him.

"This does not matter, perhaps," he continued after he had blown out the smoke and returned the calumet. "It is good for young men to be angry sometimes. But now there is something more. There is great danger now, greater than any of the young men think. There is a very old cult..."

He stopped again, and met the young man's clear, direct gaze. Yes, he knew he could trust this pupil of his old friend. He could tell in the eyes. The eyes never lied. This one would one day be one of the very great ones. He did not hesitate to tell the boy the story.

"It is called the Cult of the Vulture. The Death-bird. It is very old, older even than the worship of the Thunderbird. Its members are said to adorn themselves with vulture feathers and to slash their victims' eyes out with talons. The talons are taken from the giant bird itself, or else they are made out of silver. The followers of the Deathbird are devoted to the worship only of killing, and they kill with joy—without mercy or plan. The Deathbird demands much blood, and these madmen are eager to supply it.

"They are clever, moreover, and I am afraid that they will try to persuade our young men to join them in a great final war against the white man. They try this every year, but until last year I have always been able to talk the young men out of joining the cult. But times grow harder, and they are tired of listening to me. I fear that this year some of the Vulture people will succeed in convincing them. If they succeed, then they could well succeed in accomplishing what all of Custer's cavalry could not: destroying all the Indian nations for good."

Dire Wolf leaned back slightly and narrowed his grey eyes to sight out of the smoke hole at the peak of the tipi. "It is almost midnight," he said. "If they are coming, they will come soon."

Lin Fong raised an eyebrow. "They will come here?"

Dire Wolf nodded gravely. "I am the last of the shamans whose duty it was in the old days to take charge of the ceremonies of the Thunderbird. Perhaps it is only a foolish rivalry, but the Vulture people have always hated the Thunderbird medicine men more than anyone else. More, I think, even than the white men. So if they come tonight, they will come here. That"—his old eyes narrowed with what might have been either humor or pain—"is why you are here."

Lin's eyes widened in surprise; then he nodded his respect and allegiance once more. "If I may be of service, I am pleased that chance has brought me to your lodge at a favorable moment."

"Chance?" Dire Wolf's eyes sparkled. "Perhaps."

Lin returned the old man's smile. The firelight lit up his face. To his left the flap of the tipi fluttered slightly. Lin was not sure whether Dire Wolf had noticed the tiny motion, but it was all the young Master needed. His body tensed for fight. He inhaled once, slowly and deep.

Before he had released the breath the quiet was cut by the sound of tearing cloth. A huge curved blade slashed through the tent, and the young man who would soon be known as the world's greatest Master of Kung Fu was on his feet even before his brain had acknowledged the attacker's presence.

The tent split wide and a black figure leaped in, the blade whirling before him. The man was naked except for a tightly-worn loincloth and a mammoth headdress on top of which a second silver crescent, nearly as large as the one in his hand, shone madly in the firelight. His face and body had been rubbed all over with pitch, and on his arms and chest Vermillion streaks spoke the language of war.

The man rushed in a frenzy toward the seated shaman. Dire Wolf did not move. His old eyes went wide in surprise and what looked to Lin Fong like dull recognition, but he remained sitting, as if awaiting the inevitable.

But the young Master jumped. In a second he had placed himself between the old man and the attacker, and his arms were weaving sinuously before him in a light defensive dance.

The sickle came down in a swoop at the intruder. Lin met the descending arm cleanly and the blade flicked off to the side. He stepped back to receive another charge, and the black figure stepped back also.

This time the blade came up from the left, barely missing Lin's exposed belly. The young man stepped back gracefully and, just as the gleaming silver passed in front, sent a crushing Buffalo Horn at the attacker's wrist. The man was fast, and the blow glanced off, bruising but not breaking the bone.

Now the black figure began to use the vicious weapon like a baton. It twirled faster and faster in the firelight, gathering speed as it approached the young man's eyes, until, a foot from his face, it was only a blur of deadly metal. Lin Fong did not move. He gauged exactly where the steel would strike and waited.

Then the headdress bobbed so slightly that only the keen eyes of the young Master caught the movement. He shifted his weight to the left and watched the singing sickle dart an inch from his right side.

His left arm came up in a long glide to deliver a Pounding Wave to the side of the black figure's head. The man pivoted on his heels and backed off to the edge of the tent. Lin pursued him with a series of Ram's Heads, but he could not get through the flailing steel. He shifted his weight again and his right foot lanced out in a long, precise Lightning Kick, but again the attacker pivoted and the kick fell short.

The man was fast, there was no doubt about that. He was no simple assassin who struck cleanly and ran. He had done this kind of fighting before, and he knew his weapon well. While Lin was having some difficulty maneuvering in the tight, smoky space, the man seemed entirely at home. Now he rested against the side of the tent, the blade still a blur before him. He seemed to expend no effort to move the blade; it was alive, it moved of its own accord...

But it was only a sickle. And a sickle was not enough to send against the perfectly trained body of the young Blue Circle Master. Lin approached the waiting figure, and this time it was he who attacked.

A Dragon Stamp straight on forced the man to lower his guard and that left his face unprotected. Lin's Tiger Claw leaped out, and two streaks of blood joined the red paint on the man's body. The Master's Knife Slash struck down from the left and, when the target dodged, he sent a withering Lightning Kick into his side.

Now the attacker's blade slowed. He was against the wall, and he knew that he was suddenly in trouble. Never before had he seen hands this fast. Never before had he met such calm determination in the eyes of his victims. His expression grew agitated, he wavered, and Lin saw that now he could finish him.

He did not wish to kill him if he could help it. He would pull the next kick slightly, and it would knock the wind out of the man. He would place the foot just below the rib cage. He turned his powerful body to the right, braced himself, took air into his lungs.

The old man who had been, throughout the attack, sitting quietly a few feet away, sensed the coming attack. Now he moved slightly in the earth. The faint noise alerted the young Master, and he withheld his attack for a moment. There was something wrong. He sensed that Dire Wolf was trying to tell him something.

But he could not hear it. Could not listen.

Not now. After he had struck, then...

7

The old man's mouth opened. His voice quaked. "No," he was saying. "Do not..."

Lin hesitated. And in that second of doubt the silver blade struck out again. This time it laced a thin line of blood down the Master's arm, and from behind him Lin heard a quick intake of breath from Dire Wolf.

The Vulture figure came on. Lin backstepped around the fire, his arms a delicate shield of Swooping Birds and Whipping Branches.

In a moment he was facing Dire Wolf, and the black figure was between them. The old man's face showed what Lin had not seen on it in all the days he had spent here. It was not fear, exactly, at least not fear for himself. Confusion, apprehension, a kind of blind unspecified terror... his features seemed to be set in a peculiar wince, as if, whatever the outcome of the fight might be, it could only bring him pain.

Lin was on the far side of the fire. The shining blade still moved rapidly in front of the painted figure. Suddenly it stopped. Lin got ready to spring, but in that moment the air was filled with a shower of sparks and burning twigs. All before him was a cloud of flame from where the attacker's foot had kicked upward through the fire toward the young Master.

Lin began to drop back, shielding his face from the flying embers with his hands, but at the same instant he saw the Vulture's assassin whirl on the other side of the fire and sweep the long curved steel savagely down toward the puzzled face of his friend. The diversion had been successful. It had given the attacker the second he needed to complete the mission he had been sent here for. With mounting horror Lin saw the blade flash and descend toward the old man's eyes.

The young Master had no time to think. His body reacted with the blinding speed of a leaping cat.

And this time it was a leap to the death. His mind could no longer afford an instant's hesitation. Every tingling muscle of his body went into action, strained over the space between him and the blade.

He was in the air, his long, lean body stretched flat out over the coals of the fire. He sailed, a deadly lance, toward the head of the man who threatened his friend. The blade came down like lightning, but the foot of the Master cracked an instant faster, and the deadly silver flew harmlessly into the skin wall of the tent.

The Master's left foot carried through to the attacker's temple, splitting the skull in a long hairline fissure. This time there was no time to pull the leg back. This time his attacker lay in a small cloud of blood at his feet.

The old man lifted himself wearily from his sitting position and leaned over the still form of the man who had just tried to kill him. Over his face came an expression of immense grief; then the moment passed and the calm that Lin had become accustomed to seeing there took its place. He looked up from the body and faced the young Master. His kind grey eyes expressed a painful thanks. It was obvious that he knew Lin could have done nothing else.

"When you moved a moment ago," the young Master said, "I knew you did not want him killed. I did not wish it either. But when he struck at you, I could not take the chance of only wounding him."

"You do not have to say it," said the old man. "I understand."

Lin met the Indian's eyes, and watched the grief there ebb and flow like the water of a summer stream. "Did you know him well?" he asked.

Dire Wolf was again motionless. His eyes closed briefly as if in prayer. Then he faced the boy. Again his voice was strong.

"He was my son."

CHAPTER ONE. *THE INITIATE*

In the middle of the great American desert called Death Valley National Monument there are sporadic outcroppings of red rock which the harsh winds have not yet reduced to sand. These jagged sentinels dot the barren landscape in irregular patterns from horizon to horizon, shielding gila monsters and prairie dogs from the merciless heat, reflecting sunrise and sunset like an army of dull red mirrors, casting streaks of shadow across the thin band of asphalt that takes an occasional hardy motorist through the valley that the locals call "the hottest place this side of Hell." In one of these towers of rock there is a cleft slightly less than six feet high and not much more than a foot wide—an easy passage for reptiles seeking shade, and just wide enough for a slender and agile person to squeeze through. Beyond the cleft, inside the tower, there is a small cave, guarded from the sunshine by a large overhang of red rock above the cleft, so that the inside is always utterly black.

Except for once each year. Exactly at midday on the day of the Autumn Equinox, a shaft of sunlight cuts through a hole the size of a dime in the roof of the cave and, for a few brief moments, illuminates a spot no bigger than a man's eye on the cavern floor. For that fraction of a minute each year the inside of the cave is faintly light, and it is possible to make out the contours of the tiny cavern. A person whom chance had brought through the cleft at just that moment in the celestial year would be able to see that the cave is roughly circular, and that the walls rise smoothly into a dome perhaps twenty feet from the cool rock floor. He would see that the walls are painted with strange devices similar in appearance both to Egyptian hieroglyphics and to Chinese characters. He would see that, into the hard floor of the cavern, a human hand had scratched a perfect circle about a dozen feet in diameter. And he would see, in the moment the pinpoint of light cut through the dome, that the thin ray of sunshine came to rest on the cavern floor in the exact center of that circle.

If he looked at the legends painted around him, he would recognize no known human language. If he inspected the circle at his feet, he would find nothing more than a series of unevenly spaced lines scratched into the stone across the circumference of the circle. If he looked at the spot illuminated by the ray of sunlight, he would notice only a slight indentation in the rock.

He might wonder at the strangeness of it for the few seconds the cavern was lit up. Then the sun would inch toward the West, and for another twelve months the cave would again be dark as a grave.

The sands, that stretch away from this singular outcropping are dotted by several hundred other out-croppings as well; to the few travellers who cross the desert each month in search of stories and photographs, none of these masses of weathered stone seems different from any other. Perhaps some are more grotesquely carved by centuries of wind; perhaps some throw off the reds and oranges of the dying suns with special piquancy. These the travellers bring back with them to Bell and Howell projectors in Sioux City and Jersey City and Jacksonville. But no traveller suspects, as his car speeds through the enervating haze of the valley, that one of the stone giants houses, in darkness, a rough-hewn temple dedicated to the service of a Power whose worship is older than that of Jesus or Mohammed or Buddha or even the ancient Americans' Thunderbird.

Even the Indians who live today in the small California and Nevada towns on the border of Death Valley know nothing of the cave. For the tribal legends have not been told around their fires for over two generations, and even the oldest men—those who might have heard of Custer's defeat from their grandfathers who had been there—have no knowledge of the location, or even the existence, of the cave that their most ancient ancestors called the Devil's Hole.

So the cavern sits unseen and undisturbed in the middle of the wilderness, its only residents the vermin of the desert, its only link to the world of human kind the undecipherable symbols scratched in its walls three thousand years before Columbus.

On a Friday afternoon in the late summer of 1963, that was about to change.

A hundred yards from the rock tower a large black vulture sat on a second tower and scanned the desert for signs of death. He had been waiting all afternoon and he was hungry. His eyes narrowed and swept the sand anxiously as the sun dipped toward the horizon.

At dusk the vulture's keen sight picked up a small motion at the mouth of the rock cleft. He raised his huge wings slowly and then let them drop, readying himself for flight.

But what he saw told him that there would be no scavenging for him here. It was no stray prairie dog who had caught the bird's eye, no snake slithering toward dinner or death.

It was Man. A hundred yards away, the vulture watched with interest as the form emerged from the fissure in the rock. The vulture had never seen a man come out of there before, and he narrowed his eyes further to take in the curiosity.

The man was short and slim. His head bore a crown of what might have been hair or black straw, and his face was covered with it also. His form was black all over, except that from his shoulders there hung a long purplish cloak, and from around his neck swayed something that flashed silver in the twilight. He drew his body out of the rock and turned almost casually to inspect his surroundings. As he did so, the falling sun caught the bright object around his throat and a piercing white light passed like a searchlight up to where the bird was sitting.

The vulture twitched.

He had seen searchlights before. With them came the roar of bounty hunters' guns.

He had seen enough. With a haughty squawk he rose off his rock and wheeled away from the man into the desert.

The man's face turned up at the sound. He raised his arms in what might have been either a challenge or a salute, and his dark, small features winced into a grin. Then he let his arms fall and started to walk.

He walked five miles due West. By the time he reached the asphalt ribbon that cut the barren valley in two, it was dark. He crossed the highway and walked another mile West to a large outcropping of black rock that loomed like a ghostly castle against the last flickers of the buried sun. He walked around the rock and smiled as the trim black body of a new Mercedes SL met his eyes.

Good, he thought. Just where Kak said it would be.

He opened the unlocked door and eased his body into the leather seat. His hand found the ignition key in the lock. He turned it and the powerful motor whirred, ready. Then he slammed the door and floored the accelerator.

The Mercedes shot out from behind the rock and s. . . a wide circle, throwing out a fountain of sand toward the . . . wheels hit the highway with a soft bump.

The car sped South for two hours until the street lights of small towns and the headlights of traffic told the black-clad driver he was nearing Los Angeles. Just before he reached Barstow the man screeched the powerful car to a halt. He reached to his neck and unclasped the heavy brooch that held the purple cloak closed, drew the rich material off his shoulders and placed it gently on the seat beside him. He pulled open the collar of his black turtleneck and tucked the silver object inside. Then he withdrew a pair of Air Force sunglasses from the glove compartment and put them on.

The car shot South again. It moved onto the Barstow Freeway and at Colton shifted to the San Bernadino, heading West. It sped past the concrete and plastic and steel of a thousand apartment complexes until it reached the center of the city of Los Angeles. There it took the cutoff for the Hollywood Freeway and headed Northwest through the San Fernando Valley. It passed the Hollywood Bowl and Universal Studios and the hundreds of cheap strip joints that flourished that summer around the world's entertainment capital. The driver's small dark eyes stayed fixed on the road signs ahead; he seemed not to notice the neon advertisements inviting him to sample the myriad delights of the new Babylon.

At Victory Boulevard the Mercedes left the freeway and headed West toward the comfortable singles bars and lowrise dwellings of Van Nuys. It turned right on Sepulveda Boulevard, right again, then left, and pulled to a stop before a low pink building with a close-cropped lawn and false Ionian pillars flanking the door.

The man from the desert stepped out of the car holding the folded cloak in one hand. He shut the door quietly and looked at the house. The letters Four-Two-One rose in script from the pink stucco front.

He walked the twenty feet to the doorway and inspected the ten names near a row of buzzers. Then he rang all but one of them and waited. In a second a gaggle of voices responded.

"Where's the party?" he said quietly. His voice was soft, nearly apologetic.

There was a moment of silence and then the buzzer sounded and the man walked in. As the voices resumed behind him, he smiled at the simple ruse. There's always a party somewhere, he chuckled.

14

The man climbed the stairs to the second floor and stopped before a pale green door with the number 5 in red beside it. From his trousers pocket he withdrew a set of skeleton keys and began trying them on the lock. As the click of the fourth key told him the tumblers had caught, he glanced up and down the hall quickly. Nothing. He entered the apartment and closed the door behind him.

He crossed the large central room in the darkness and opened a sliding glass door to a private patio. Water dribbled from a plaster cherub's mouth into a small basin. Palm fronds swayed in the night breeze. The man unfolded the cloak and put it on. He retrieved the silver object from behind his turtleneck and let it hang free. Then he seated himself in a webbed deck chair, placed the sunglasses on the metal arm, and waited. Somewhere a bell tolled.

It was Saturday.

"Goddamned landlord!"

Patricia "Boomers" Keele cursed softly as the key stuck again. Four six-day weeks in a row were too much for any working girl, and when the work was topless dancing in one of North Hollywood's raunchiest night spots, a girl had earned a weekend's rest. She jiggled the key again but nothing happened.

This she didn't need. Tuesday she had told that bastard about the lock. Here it was Friday. No, Saturday. And still stuck.

She laid the groceries on the mat and put both hands to the job. This time there was a small click and the key twisted slightly to the right. Patricia breathed her relief and pushed.

The door swung in and the package which had been resting against it followed. The girl lunged for it a second too late, and groaned as the half-dozen loose eggs she had just picked up at the all-night Farmers' Market toppled out onto the rug.

She dragged the other bag into the apartment and slammed the door. Then she gathered together everything but the broken eggs and went to the kitchen. She laid the two packages on the counter and returned to the living room with a sponge.

"Well, it could be worse," she muttered as pieces of shell and yolk oozed out of the bag onto the green Oriental carpet. She rubbed briskly and rose with the sodden sponge in one hand and the dripping bag in the other. "Three left. Enough for an omelet, anyway."

In the kitchen she set the three good eggs aside and threw out the broken ones, Then she flicked on the radio and began to unpack the rest of the groceries. Thank God for Mrs. Swanson, she thought as she placed the weekend's allotment of TV dinners in the freezer. They weren't exactly her idea of a gourmet feast—more like glue and cardboard actually, she thought with grim amusement—but when you ate supper at three in the morning and breakfast while everybody else in L.A. was guzzling Happy Hour Martinis you didn't have time to whip up Tournedos Rossini.

It was a balmy late summer night in 1963, and a new English rock group called The Beatles was singing a song called "I Wanna Hold Your Hand." Patricia's hand hit the dial in unconscious exasperation. It wasn't that she didn't like the song—it was catchy enough, and she sort of liked that one they called Paul, he reminded her of her kid brother Bo—but when you came home to the peace of your own apartment, you just didn't want to hear the same stuff you had been dancing to all week long.

She turned the dial until the rich baritone she had fallen in love with almost ten years ago, back in Oklahoma, began to resonate among the four walls of the dinette.

Elvis.

Now that was when music was music. None of the college kids that frequented The Catpatch could stand him. Figured. Jealous little boys, that was all. With their tongues lolling out of their mouths every time she stepped on stage, like they'd never seen a tit before. And wouldn't know what to do with it anyway, if it was handed to them on a platter.

Well, that was all over now for another three days. Three days of peace and quiet. No dirty old men and no dirty young men and no more of that damn dyke Sandie offering to help her off with her bra—Christ, she was glad to be shut of the lot of them! Just a few bottles of beer and some old movies and Elvis on the box and lots of well-deserved sleep.

She pried the six cans of Coors out of their plastic jacket, fit them into the door of the refrigerator, and closed the door. Now for some eggs and bed.

She was glad she had told Don she could not attend the meeting. He had been angry, of course, but after all he wasn't an unreasonable guy, and when she had explained that she would simply be too tired to receive the spirits properly, he had mumbled that he understood and agreed to give the Central Circle the bad news.

Patricia put a pot of water on for coffee and reflected on the odd turn of events that had, in the last six months, brought her to her present bizarre eminence among the spiritualist sects of Southern California.

When she had come to Los Angeles from her native Oklahoma five years ago, she never had a clue that she was in any way different from a thousand other pretty girls come to seek their fortunes in the big city. She thought herself lucky then to land a waitressing job that paid sixty bucks a week after tips. In 1958 she had not dared hope for more than that. The Big Break would come sooner or later, she believed, and she would be up on the silver screen alongside Marilyn and the other greats. In the meantime it was all she could do to pay the rent in a tiny walk-up over in North Hollywood. So she dreamed and hoped that by the next year she would have saved enough to start acting lessons, and put in her fifty hours a week, and was grateful to do it because she had finally escaped the drudgery of small-town life. She was in the big city now, and soon she would be in the big time.

It went on like that for three years. Then she met Don Blake, and it didn't take the enterprising young writer long to sift her out from the thousands of others in just her situation—not long at all to spot her particular talents.

"You've got a special gift, honey, a very special gift. You must share it with the world."

Patricia smiled warmly in recall as she saw his handsome ruddy face again, delivering that surprising message to her for the first time. He was the first man who had ever looked at her without undisguised lust, the first whose eyes had seemed to rest not just on the substantial bosom which had given her the nickname she hated, but on her very soul. Don's eyes had glowed with a strange fire that night, and Patricia recalled fondly how easy it had been for her to believe the odd things he was saying. It had seemed, as he spoke, that his voice was not quite human but came from far away. And it had seemed the most natural thing in the world for her to assent to do as he said, and to find herself later that night giving another one of her gifts, this one perhaps not so special, to the man who was about to change her life.

The next morning, with her small daybed folded back into place, she drank coffee and heard Don explain his great plan for her.

"Very few people are blessed in the way you are blessed, Patricia. Only to a handful of human creatures do the Lords of Light grant the visions that will soon be yours. You are now what the adepts call a primary initiate, but soon you will pass the first stage of your initiation and be admitted to a small and select circle, the circle of those to whom it is vouchsafed to see and guard the one pure and white light. The marriage of Heaven and Hell we will show you, Patricia, the union of all things dark and light, the coming of a kingdom of surpassing majesty such as the world has never before seen. In that kingdom the lion and the lamb will be one, and the Lord of Darkness will take his rightful place beside the Lords of Light, and the world will be gathered anew. And in that kingdom, Patricia"—his voice hushed with emotion, and the girl was spellbound—"you will be the Priestess who calls the Gathering in."

Then Don described how she would be required, for the next year or two, to attend a weekly meeting of the group he called the Gathering, and how at the end of this period of training and study and mutual worship, she would become one of them—indeed, she would become their queen.

"That day," he pronounced solemnly, "will be the most important day of your life."

Patricia had heard and believed and joined. The following day Don took her for the first time to the group called the Gathering, and at the end of the meeting she was entirely convinced. By the end of the week she had given herself over completely to the group, and had entered a new realm of experience. A second world opened out for her. She was no longer simply Patricia Keele, twenty-three year old waitress; now she was also Lilith 3, novitiate priestess of the Order of the Last Reaping. She attended the weekly Gatherings devotedly, participated in the group's communal sexual activities without hesitation or embarrassment, learned the tenets of the Order's creed in the original arcane language, walked the Strip twice a week recruiting new followers. Once she had even presided at a midnight service, and Don—or rather Malachi 7, as he was known in the Gathering—said she had performed admirably.

It was very exciting for the girl from Oklahoma. In two years she had risen rapidly in the Order and, as Don had predicted, she had risen in her "earthly" life as well. The Catpatch, to be sure, was no Copacabana, but it was a hell of a cut above Jim's Beanery where she had been slinging hash only months before. It was nice to be able to afford an occasional steak, to be able to furnish her apartment with something other than Salvation Army rejects, to be able to say fuck-off to the heavy tippers who figured that their money bought them the dancer as well as the dance.

She was pleased at how it had gone. And there was more to come,-she was sure of that. She believed in Don—or in Malachi 7—and she believed in the Order, and in two years she had never missed a meeting.

Until tonight.

She cracked the three eggs a little sharply and watched them run into the bowl. Her hand moved in quick small circles as the whisk turned the eggs into an even pale yellow. Then she turned on the burner, placed the small pan over the flame, and threw in a dash of oil.

She knew she should not be upset about missing the Gathering. Don had said if she were that tired, it would be all right. He would inform the Central Circle and it would be all right. She fingered the silver symbol she always wore under her clothing—the small shiny item that even went into her bikini panties when she was dancing topless—as if trying to draw from it the protective magic she needed to quell the anxiety rising inside her.

What if the Central Circle did not understand? Don had always impressed upon her the importance of constant diligence, of continual adherence to the rules of the Order, lest unseen forces wean her away from the true path of enlightenment... and attendance at the weekly meetings was one of the principal rules. Idly, but with a growing unease, she wondered if by missing this one meeting in two years she had let herself in for any danger.

No. Enough of that kind of thinking. The Circle would understand and everything would be fine. She would go again next week and it would all be fine. She brushed a strand of black hair out of her eye and threw the eggs into the pan.

They crackled and spat. Patricia reached for a spatula and began to shirr them quickly, before they could stick. Elvis had stopped singing and an old Brenda Lee song added its plaintive

19

tones to the noise from the stove. Patricia smiled. Elvis and now Brenda Lee. It was going to be a fine night.

She took a plate from the pinewood cupboard above the stove and laid it on the counter. Then she gave the omelet a last flick and eased it onto the plate. She turned off both burners and spooned a teaspoonful each of instant coffee and cream into a cup, then filled it with the steaming water. Then she took a fork and knife from the drawer beneath the counter and carried her breakfast-supper to the dining alcove.

Dining alcove. The name always made her chuckle. The cheap bastard she rent from threw up a six-foot piece of plywood between the stove and the living room door and charged ten dollars more on the rent. Well, that was the price you paid for getting out of the slums.

She sat and ate greedily. She hoped Don wouldn't call now. She couldn't handle any callers now, not even on the phone. Tonight she just wanted to be alone. John Wayne on the tube, that was the limit of company for tonight.

Patricia finished the eggs and lit a cigarette. The coffee steamed invitingly before her. She took her time, enjoying each drag, each sip, listening with growing appreciation as her played-out body relaxed to the country music on the radio. Yeah. It would be fine. The Circle would understand, and she'd go again next week.

She finished the cigarette, flicked off the radio in the middle of a Flatt and Scruggs ramble, hit the light, and crossed to her bedroom.

She pushed open the door and flicked on the light next to the unmade double bed. It was the little things, she thought, that would drive you crazy. With one less day of work a week she'd have the little extra energy it would take to straighten out the spread and sheets.

And to remember to draw those damn drapes! Angrily she crossed to the sliding door and drew the fabric together. There were enough peeping Toms in L.A. to start their own union, and the last thing they needed was encouragement.

She pushed on the TV and began taking off her clothes. She pulled the light shift over her head and sat on the bed to work off the snug panty-hose. Then she unhooked her bra and her large breasts fell free. Finally she hooked a finger inside the elastic of her panties and pulled. She kicked the clothing vaguely toward the closet and for a second stood quietly in the middle of the room. As the TV came up to cast grey light on her full, sensuous body, she thought of what a pleasure it was to be naked when you didn't have a hundred horny eyes watching your every movement.

Only John Wayne, she chuckled. She turned up the sound and flipped the dial until the Duke's craggy face filled the screen. Then she crossed the room again and entered the bathroom. One hand hit the shower knob while the other fumbled for the makeup remover pads.

By the time the mascara had disappeared into the sink the water was hot and Patricia was ready. She stepped into the tile enclosure with a mixture of anticipation and uneasiness, as if she were a demure bride looking forward to her deflowering. The water ran down her body in full smooth sheets. The girl shook her head happily, grabbed for the soap, lavished it on her weary skin. For a full ten minutes she let the water play with her, smiling as the tightness of a week's dancing left her in a rising cloud of steam. Then she shut off the tap and stepped dripping out of the stall. She grabbed a huge orange towel from the rack and walked into her bedroom moving it lustily over her skin.

John Wayne was shooting Apaches.

The man who had come from the desert rose slowly from the deck chair. His long cloak hung straight behind him in the stillness as he placed the sunglasses in his hip pocket, breathed the night air, and smiled. The three hours' sleep had done him good. And Kak had said it might be as long as five, so he was way ahead of schedule. He was glad the girl had not made him wait long.

The man slid the glass door back quietly and reentered the living room. Then he turned left and stood lazily with one shoulder resting against the jamb of the bedroom doorway. For a minute he watched Patricia dry herself in front of the television. He was no voyeur, and certainly he already had more women at his disposal than he really wanted; but this was a special case, and besides the girl pleased him. He liked the way the cheeks of her ass shook as the towel attacked her hair. He watched, silent.

John Wayne disappeared abruptly and was replaced by the effusive, unguent voice of Ralph Williams. The girl turned down the volume of the set and the man behind her spoke softly. "Nice. Very nice."

Patricia whirled, her face blanched with fear. She clutched the big towel defensively to her as she appraised the intruder. Quickly she took in his easy stance, the black clothing, the cloak, the thin, nearly friendly smile.

No, he did not look like a rapist. She stuttered, feigning bravado. "What the hell do you want?"

The narrow, small-featured face of the man from the desert broke into a grin. His slightly aquiline nose twitched as if he were a beast on the scent. His lips turned up, nearly baring his teeth. His eyes seemed to sparkle with an unnatural fire as he spoke. "Why, you, of course, my pretty Lilith." Lilith. He had called her Lilith. Then he must be from the Order. Maybe from the Central Circle, even. Torn between relief that she was not going to be raped and apprehension over the unexpected visit from a creature who might have far worse threats than rape at his disposal, Patricia shut off the TV behind her and faced the man squarely. His face was immobile, and it betrayed just the hint of a tenuous, sardonic smile. She waited for him to speak—to give an appraisal or a judgment, she did not know which. Then she noticed something. It was the device which hung from the intruder's neck. Like the one that hung from her own, it was deep burnished silver, and like her own it swung easily, heavily, seeming to catch all the mystical currents of the universe and diffuse them out into the small space between them with a pale, shimmering aura.

But unlike hers, the man's pendant was not in the shape of an inverted Cross. It was rougher, more twisted, as if the metal had been subjected to an unbelievable heat and had shriveled up in rebellion. It held a ghastly kind of beauty for the girl as she watched it sway against the black of the man's sweater. Gradually the shape of the object became clear and she could make out what it was.

Four arms, like the cross. But each one curved maliciously, curved and sharpened.

It was a claw of some kind. The claw of a giant bird of prey. A talon.

Patricia could not keep her eyes off it. It was as if the shaped metal emanated a delicious and irresistible poison which, sooner or later, she would have to taste. The light that came off the talon was not simply the light reflected from the night lamp near her bed. It was unlike any light she had ever seen before. It seemed to bore into her soul. It illuminated all things. It laid bare all secrets. It was, she suddenly realized, the one pure white light of which Malachi 7—of which the Central Circle itself—had spoken.

Was this her time, then? Was this the time of her investiture? Or of her undoing?

Patricia didn't know. She knew nothing except that, whatever this man told her, she would believe. Whatever he bid her do, that she would do.

His voice was still soft, and he seemed to read her thoughts. "That is right, Lilith. Your time has arrived. Watch the talon. In time it will tell you all things."

Patricia heard the voice as if from far away. It seemed to come through a thousand walls to lay before her an absolute, undeniable command. Gradually she lost control of her body and, like a sign the towel dropped before her to the floor. The man's gaze ran up and down the white skin briefly, and then he spoke again.

"Dress yourself, woman. We are going."

"Going?" A last vestige of earthly rationality made the girl inquire softly, "Where?"

The response came like the sound of a gigantic bell.

"It is called the. Devil's Hole. We are going to Kak Nan Tang."

CHAPTER TWO. *EVERY NUT IN THE COUNTRY*

"There's no such thing as an accident." Lieutenant Ben Spencer was annoyed. The series of ritualistic slayings that his men had been uncovering in the Los Angeles hills in the last month had him puzzled. Twenty years on the force had convinced him that a group of crimes meant a pattern of crimes, and here he could find no pattern. No M.O., as the boys in Homicide would say. He looked pointedly at his partner Joe Corcoran and repeated the phrase that had long ago made him laughingstock, hero, and all-round enigma to his buddies in the department.

"There's got to be a pattern." Joe shrugged and pulled the trigger of the heavy regulation Magnum. The explosion reverberated deafeningly through the corridor. Thirty yards away a man with a gun pointed at the two police officers twitched violently, a huge round slug through his heart. Lieutenant Corcoran pulled the trigger again. And again. The figure jerked twice more. "Pull that thing up here, will you, Joe?" Corcoran smiled as though he knew what his partner was about to say, but complied indulgently with the request. Spence could use a little humoring, after all. He motioned to the operator and the machine clattered to life, jerking the cardboard target toward the two men like a great crippled bird. When it reached the firing line Corcoran pulled it off the snap and waved his thanks to the man in the booth. Then he handed the target to his partner and raised an eyebrow.

"Well, Sherlock, what do you find here?"

Spencer took the six-foot piece of paper arid folded it rapidly three times so that the target area over the heart was exposed in a one-foot square. He placed his finger methodically, quizzically, in each of the three closely placed holes. Two of them had pierced the valentine at the center. One was a half inch out. Joe was a good man with an iron, no doubt of it.

"Now this here," he said quietly, "is a pattern. But it's not complete, see?"

Spencer pointed to the shy mark. "This hole here, it's trying its damnedest to get in to the pattern, but it's not quite making it. Not yet. When it makes it, you'll have a perfect round, Joseph. And I'll have my case."

Corcoran smiled. "Spence, did it ever occur to you that two out of three still means the guy is just as dead as the coroner wants him?"

His partner returned the smile. "It occurred to me. But I leave that kind of shit to the Homicide boys. Simple minds, you know. Me, I'm a detective. They put me on the Kink Squad because I'm good at seeing things that other folks miss. The long shots in the crossword puzzles, you know. So I got to keep at it, Joe. Got to find it. Come on, I'll buy you a cup of coffee. We got to meet that damn Chinese kid in an hour."

"Josie's?"

"Yeah."

They walked up the stairs of the pistol range and turned toward the greasy spoon around the corner from me station. Corcoran let his partner muse. They had been friends a long time, and he knew there were times you just had to let Ben Spencer have his head to himself. Besides, one of them had to keep an eye out for trouble while the "detective" did his Deep Thoughts routine. They walked in silence.

Spencer was not happy with how the case was going. Three killings in less than a month, and still no real clues.

It was not that he was upset about the murders themselves. He had been on the force long enough not to be shocked at anything as simple as murder—even the bizarre kinds of murders his fellow Californians seemed to be addicted to. He'd seen it all: those two years on Homicide had given him the stomach for anything these weirdoes could dish out.

But he didn't like these killings. He didn't like them at all. They were too chaotic, too purposeless even for Los Angeles. They tore at something deep inside him, something deeper than sympathy or pain.

He reviewed the gruesome details.

A month ago Cheeka, the Los Angeles Zoo's prize baby chimp—the first to be born there in over a decade—had been abducted. Spencer remembered the newscast, with the tearful trainer pointing to the bars of the cage, pried out of shape by persons or forces unknown. Two days later the chimp's body had been found by some kids in the hills above Burbank. It had been castrated and its genitals stuffed in its mouth. This particular gruesome detail had been kept from the press, but the boys at the L.A. *Times* had man-

26

aged to discover that Cheeka's body had been staked out as in some old Indian torture—the chimp's four limbs secured by twine to tent pegs pounded into the earth at the four corners of a square. And that the animal's eyes had been ripped out, as if by a giant scavenger. Since vultures and hawks were quite common in the hills this time of year, that last detail had simply been attributed to "natural" causes, but Spencer was not so sure.

Even the expurgated version of the story was enough for the local populace. Every dog and cat from Glendale to Santa Monica was locked indoors for a week. The *Enquirer* carried tales of the famous petsnatchers of history, et cetera et cetera. Panic in the hills. And all for a goddamned chimpanzee.

But the next victim had been human, and that one Spencer couldn't shrug off. If Cheeka had been for him only the latest victim in a pretty long list of sacrificed animals—kids were constantly turning up goats' heads and dogs' guts in the hills—the body of Linda Spengler had made him think twice.

The twenty-two-year-old girl had been a schoolteacher down in Mendocino. The last year she had been hanging out with a bunch of hippies in Laurel Canyon, and two weeks ago she had reaped the bitter harvest of that association. A few of her friends, it turned out, had been what they called Sun Worshippers, and they, on their own admission, had done Linda in as a sacrifice to their god. Her heart had been ripped out while she was still alive, they said, and then cooked in a big stone burner, the kind Spencer's daughter Mary had brought back a couple of summers ago from Mexico. The sun worshippers were in custody now, pending psychiatric examination, and Spencer cursed silently as they entered Josie's. Some hotshit shrink would be sure to get the pricks off.

"One black, one no sugar." Josie's lilting Mexican voice welcomed them as she placed their regular orders before them and went back to the grill. She knew when to leave these two alone.

Spencer sipped at the black liquid and thought of the third murder. A double, this one had been, and only a week ago. No clues yet. He had the boys checking the Strip for stoolies, but nobody had sung yet.

Jamie and Melissa Strong. Young marrieds. Nice kids, everybody said. No weird ideas, no drugs, no occultist leanings. Not very "hip".

But very dead.

27

Apparently they had gone walking in the hills south of Altadena sometime last Friday. They were never seen alive again. A caretaker at the Rose Bowl found the bodies on the 50-yard line a couple of days later. Both had been slashed at the neck and about the eyes, and their naked bodies had been tied together loosely by a length of rawhide. On each of their bellies a Chinese character had been painted in their own blood. Spencer blew on the coffee and remembered what Vic Chen, the token Chinese officer in the precinct, had said about them.

"The one on the woman's belly is the symbol for autumn, or the harvest. The one on the man's represents darkness, or the color black."

Darkness. Harvest. Black autumn. None of it made a damn bit of sense. Spencer longed wryly for the good old-fashioned kind of weirdo, the kind that killed by the light of the full moon, the kind that left Tarot cards on the bodies, the kind that left various Satanist clues. He was well aware that most of the creeps he had run in in the few years he had headed the Kink Squad were what the shrinks euphemistically called "disturbed" individuals. He was aware that a great deal of psychological literature suggested that these creeps actually went out of their way to leave clues, because deep down they wanted to be caught and punished. If that was so, then Spencer's rep as ace weirdo-finder was a little overblown, but that didn't bother him half as much as the knowledge that in the present case—or cases—he was almost entirely at sea.

The evidence of a calculated, unified effort linking the various killings was flimsy at best—slashings were so common in L.A. that if you started putting things together that way soon every revenge knifing downtown would be put at the door of some demented genius. No, there was not really a lot to go on. And yet Spencer felt it, felt it strong and without the least reservation: somewhere there was a pattern. Somehow Cheeka and Linda Spengler and the Strongs and Lord knew what slaughtered innocents to come were linked together.

He didn't go along with the D.A.'s office, which was calling the Spengler case closed because a bunch of blown-out hippies had said they suddenly felt like cooking up one of their friends.

There was more to it. A lot more.

Spencer couldn't put his finger on it, but he knew that there was a single demented mind behind this new surge of savagery.

Somewhere in the hills there was a nut loose, and it was up to Spencer to find him. He sipped the coffee carefully.

There was maybe just one little clue. He had been talking to Phil Broome over at Missing Persons yesterday, and the young detective had shown him a file on a girl named Patricia Keele. A stripper. Or was it a topless dancer? "Boomers" she was called anyway, and Spencer figured that meant big tits, so it was one or the other. Broome had been doing some snooping at a place in North Hollywood called The Catpatch, where the girl worked before she disappeared a couple of days ago, and he'd found out that she was apparently a member of an occult group. High Priestess, or some shit like that. Didn't mean much—these chicks were always coming and going—except that Spencer remembered two other recent cases of the disappearance of occult group members, and putting that together with the new spate of killing, it just might point to some crazy out there trying to get all the weirdoes in town together for a concerted effort on the Establishment. "These groups are all tied in together, aren't they, Spence?" Broome had asked.

Well, Spencer didn't know. Maybe they were and then again maybe they weren't. It wouldn't hurt to check anyway. Maybe he and Joe would take a run over to the girl's apartment this afternoon.

After they got rid of the kid, that was. Christ, he wished they didn't have to meet with that one. Some crazy Chinese teenager named Chong Fei K'ing. Said he was a member of something called the Blue Circle. He had been reading the news report on the Strong murders and thought they might be able to help each other.

Another fanatic, thought Spencer. The Blue Circle. Sounded like a strip joint. And the last thing he needed right now was another teenage religious fanatic. Like that weirdo from Whittier. Said he was a Quaker, and it turned out he had killed more people than Jack the Ripper. "For the cause," he said. In his five years as head of the Special Crimes Division of the L.A. precincts, Spencer had seen them all. The boys on the beat didn't call them the Kink Squad for nothing. He was used to it, and it didn't bother him any more, not the way it had the first year. But today he'd just prefer not to. He didn't need any help from any Blue Circle, even if he was in a blind alley.

But orders were orders. Chief Jackson had made it pretty clear. "All the cooperation you can manage." All right, if that's what the old man wanted, Spencer would do his best. Probably the kid's father was a doctor. Or a politician. Played golf with Jackson. What the hell, it would only take an hour or so.

Spencer checked his watch. It was almost time. He drained the cup and looked at Corcoran. "Ready to do your bit for Chinese-American unity?"

Joe shrugged and they both got up, fumbling vaguely at their pockets.

"Forget it," Josie said.

Spencer had to admit that the handsome young Chinese sitting before him was not exactly what he had expected. The lean, muscular body was not the body of a doctor's son out for a joy-ride on the coat-tails of the force. And it was not the body of a politician's kid, either, snooping around the precinct for dirt under the pretext of offering help. Spencer decided the minute the boy strode unselfconsciously across the room and extended a firm but amiable handshake, that at the very least his first speculation had been off.

Because this K'ing character was in shape. He could see that immediately. That body was not used to tracking golf balls, or hoisting daiquiris at lawn parties. It was used to different things than that. It was used to fighting. To going for days without rest. To pushing itself beyond the point of pain.

To Kung Fu.

That's what the kid had said. Kung Fu. Well, Spencer had seen Kung Fu fighters before. Witless wonders who spent their Saturdays around the malt shops breaking bricks for their girl-friends.

But this kid was not one of them. If this kid knew Kung Fu, it was a different kind of Kung Fu than Spencer had ever seen.

Spencer found himself listening with an attention that surprised himself as the young Master told his bizarre tale. The voice was steady, expressive but even. The boy made no attempt to build himself up or to play to the sympathies of his listeners. He talked as if he were telling an old, old story that no longer needed embellishment or proof because everyone knew it was true. Spencer had ah ear for voices. If K'ing's had betrayed the slightest note of doubt or hesitation or embarrassment, Spencer would have caught it.

But no. There was nothing false here. Every crazy detail of the story came out firm and clear. If the kid was lying no lie detector in the world could have picked it up. This guy believed what he was saying.

Spencer watched the boy's face carefully, looking for the fall of an eye, the twitch of a nostril, a hand raised to scratch or brush away hair. Anything to indicate that the boy was uncomfortable with any of the details of his tale.

And again there was nothing. The deep blue eyes gazed intelligently, unwaveringly, at each of the two policemen in turn. Spencer could see that he was not trying to convince either him or Joe. He was telling a story, that was all. Whether they believed it or not seemed of little importance. *He* believed it, and that was what mattered.

Well, if even half of what the kid was saying was fact, this Kak Nan Tang character was somebody to be reckoned with.

But of course that was impossible.

No story like that could be true. The kid was sincere, but nuts, that was all. Spencer had been prepared to deal with the Blue Circle. But not a Red one too. And not an old Taoist sage who lived in the middle of the Gobi Desert teaching Kung Fu.

And certainly not a mad sorcerer named Zedak. He had seen his share of weirdoes here in L.A., but this was going a little too far.

Still, there was something about this K'ing...

When K'ing paused for a moment, Spencer took advantage of the break to turn to his partner.

"What do you think, Joe?"

Corcoran snuffed out the cigarette he had been holding and cleared his throat. He looked at K'ing.

"Well, I don't want to offend you, son, because from the way you sound I think you really believe all this stuff. But me, well, I'm from Missouri and to me it sounds a mite shaky. In fact..."

He lit another cigarette and blew the smoke out in a thin stream. "I don't buy a word of it."

K'ing's steady gaze never left the man's face. Neither of the detectives noticed the edges of his mouth curl up into the imperceptible smile of the mystic as he responded.

"That is your privilege."

Spencer spoke. He had expected a little more tact from Joe but his partner's bluntness did not surprise him. Yet he did not want their visitor to be cut off so soon, and so he broke into the silence with as much warmth as he could muster.

"Mr. K'ing, it isn't that we think you are lying. But in this business a man gets pretty skeptical."

"I can understand that."

"There is a saying that we've had to take to heart in this department. In fact you might almost call it our motto. 'If the country tilted just a little to the West, every loose nut in it would roll right into L.A.'" Spencer watched the boy's face closely as it warmed in a slight smile, but he could catch not the slightest trace of embarrassment or offense. That was good, he thought. This kid certainly had himself well in hand. "It's because of that, Mr. K'ing," he went on, "that we are apt to view your story with more than the usual degree of—let us say reserve."

"I understand," said K'ing.

"But would you go on, please, about this... this Kak Nan Tang? What does he look like?"

"He is about my height, but a little stockier. Well built, with heavy musculature. Calloused hands. Flat face. Deep black eyes. Looks a little more Chinese than me. He's two years older—twenty-one this year."

So far it sounded pretty stock to Spencer. The Villain as King Fu Fighter. "Any distinguishing marks?" he asked.

K'ing's mouth moved again. This time the faintest smile wrinkled his eyes. He placed a forefinger above each of his eyebrows and traced lines back to the hairline.

"He has scars. Two. From here... to here."

"Scars, yet!" Joe Corcoran's voice was a little raspy. He wanted to get rid of this kid quick and check out the stripper's apartment. "How did he get scars there?"

The answer was calm and, Spencer saw, entirely without pride. "I gave them to him."

Again Spencer broke in. "You say that Kak may be responsible for the ritualistic killings that have been going on the past few weeks. What makes you think so?"

K'ing leaned back in his chair. For a second he looked almost comically professorial, as if he were about to deliver an abstruse lecture to a beginning philosophy class. Then his eyes grew grave.

"It is some kind of a pattern. I have not yet been able to decipher it, but Kak is obsessed with occult patterns. In New York last year he carried out a series of brutal executions based on some very obscure Taoist texts. I was fortunate enough to find the key to the pattern before he completed the entire design, but unfortunately he was able to kill a lot of innocent people before that. I would not like to see that happen again."

Spencer's interest was caught now, and dimly he remembered the stories that had come over the wire from the East Coast about a year ago—stories of a death cult in New York that had been smashed by a young Chinese couple...

"What kind of pattern are you talking about?" he asked.

K'ing shook his head slowly back and forth. "I don't have enough to go on yet. The only thing I know for sure is that Kak's allegiance to the powers of evil is forcing him into increasingly senseless violence—his victims are unknown to him, he kills without purpose or personal interest. Also, I'm pretty sure he's somewhere in the Los Angeles area, and that if blood is being shed here, he's sure to be a part of it."

Spencer's face, drawn and faintly resigned, showed that he was unimpressed with the boy's rather vague suspicions. But it brightened as K'ing continued.

"That—and something I read in the paper. The news report said that the bodies of the young couple found in the Rose Bowl were painted with Chinese characters. Is that true?" Spencer nodded.

"Do you have a copy of those characters?" Spencer reached into the top drawer of his desk and withdrew a large manila envelope. He passed it to K'ing. "Those are the coroner's photographs. Kept from the press—you can see why. I don't suppose it would hurt for you to see them."

Spencer watched the boy open the envelope with a deft flick of a finger. He watched the clear blue eyes carefully as he pulled out the two photographs. He was still unsure about this character. He was pretty sure the kid was nuts, but how nuts he didn't know, and sometimes you could tell a lot about somebody by seeing his reaction to violence, to blood, to death.

K'ing's face never twitched as he inspected the mutilated bodies of Jamie and Melissa Strong. His first glance had told him all he wanted to know, and when the instant of recognition had gone he passed the pictures immediately back.

Only among seasoned Homicide veterans had Spencer seen the unblinking equanimity that had just been shown by this young man on encountering the photographs of the slashed bodies. Spencer stared at him with undisguised curiosity. Obviously K'ing saw more than he was saying, and Spencer figured he understood even more than he saw.

"Well?" The voice was Corcoran's. It still had an edge, but you could tell that the boy's easy absorption of the evidence had not been lost on the detective. The kid had been around killing before, that was certain. He eyed the young Chinese with a new respect.

"Well..." K'ing reached into his pocket and fingered the cloth patch he had carried all the way from North Africa. The patch with the picture of the black bird and the same Chinese characters he had just seen in the pictures. He did not remove it from his pocket.

"I have seen those two characters together once before. That time they were from Kak. It was a warning, perhaps, or a taunt, I am not sure. But I am sure it was from Kak. I did not know what it meant then and I do not know what it means now. But I know it is from Kak, and that means he is somewhere close by."

The boy's face showed a strange animation as he spoke. Spencer could see he was a young man of many different qualities. Mad he might be, but this one was no simple crackpot.

"What do they mean? The characters, I mean." Joe Corcoran's voice was direct this time. It carried a note of strident authority.

"You would translate them, I believe, as *Dark Harvest.*"

"Dark harvest—isn't that just what Vic Chen said?"

Spencer nodded and his partner's voice rose. "And how would this kid know that?" He turned to K'ing. "How do we know you're not tied in with these creeps? How do we know you're not in with your buddy Kak? How do we know you're not Kak himself?"

Spencer quieted his partner with a friendly wave of the hand. "Don't ride him, Joe." Then he turned to K'ing. The boy's oddly animated expression had not changed throughout the short interrogation. Now it softened as the older detective spoke. "How *did* you know that, son?"

K'ing smiled. "Perhaps it is not apparent to you gentlemen, but I am half Chinese. Should I not know my own language?"

Spencer returned the young Master's smile, and Corcoran too had to chuckle at his *faux pas.* "All right, all right," he said hurriedly. "Maybe I owe you an apology. And maybe not. I'll let you know."

K'ing raised a hand dismissively. "It does not matter. What matters is that Kak must be stopped."

"Well, we're all agreed on that. Kak... or whoever is responsible for the killings."

King's voice did not waver. "Kak," he repeated.

"All right. If you're so sure it's him, what do you think we should do?"

K'ing met the older man's inquisitive gaze evenly. "I have told you what I know. Is it not time that you told me what you know?"

Spencer nodded, and K'ing listened attentively while the detective relayed the lead that Phil Broome had given him about the dancer Patricia Keele. He was quiet as Spencer told him that he and his partner had planned to visit the missing girl's apartment that afternoon, as soon as K'ing had left. When Spencer had finished, he rose easily and looked amiably at the two policemen.

"Well," he said. "What are we waiting for?"

Spencer jiggled the skeleton key gently and the door came open. K'ing and Joe Corcoran followed him in. He had just got the layout of the large central living room clear in his mind when a white light flashed in front of him and he went down, a pain like an electric shock splitting his head in two.

When he woke up Joe Corcoran was leaning over him smiling.

"How you feeling, buddy?"

Spencer put a hand to his head and his eyes took in the bare walls of the hospital room.

"Head feels like it's been kicked by the proverbial horse. What the hell happened?"

"You got kicked all right, but it wasn't no horse. You'll be up in a day or two. I know it probably hurts like hell, but the doc says it didn't jar that delicate grey matter any, so you'll be O.K."

"Tell me about it."

His partner leaned back comfortably in the visitor's chair and lit a cigarette. Spencer noticed now that his right wrist was bandaged. He nodded toward it, and the glance that passed between the two friends said that Corcoran's injury would not be left out of the telling.

"It was a sight, I'm telling you, Spence. I'm real sorry you didn't get a chance to see it.

"The second we got into the stripper's room they hit. Three of them. The one that got you must have weighed say 155, but he was fast as hell and I guess you know how hard his heels are. Saw it out of the corner of my eye. He comes sailing in from the left, must have been six, maybe seven feet off the ground. *Horizontal,* you know! Foot comes out like a fucking spear. Kind of beautiful, that elevation, you know what I mean? Anyway, that must have been the last you saw."

Spencer groaned more in disgust than pain. "Shit, I didn't even see that. What then?"

"Well, the other two, they're a little slower. Not much, but enough so I'm still on my feet, see? I duck and the guy who's coming at me, his foot keeps coming and it goes right through the goddamn wall. Through the fucking wall, can you believe it! I hate to think of what my head would've looked like if the bastard had connected. The third one, he comes at the kid, and he ducks it too. You should of seen them, Spence. This was the real shit, I'm telling you. Nothing like those punks we wiped up at Alameda last year. These guys were tough. You should of seen them in the air like that, like a bunch of fucking dragons... It was a sight to see.

"Anyway, they're on their feet again before I can blink and they're backed off about five, six feet, you know? And they start circling and getting set again. You could see the veins working. They're wearing those fucking queer threads, you know? Real tight pants and that shit, only these weren't no fucking fags. They come up again with blood in their eyes. I don't mind telling you, Spence, I was scared shitless."

"What about the kid? What happened to him?" Corcoran grinned. He was going to make it last. Once a man starts on a good story, you just got to let him take his own pace. "Now don't rush me, man. I'm coming to it." He drew on the cigarette.

"Well, there we are, the kid and me. You're out and I can see those three fuckers are getting ready to jump again, and so I figure what the hell, if I don't make some kind of move fast these creeps are going to make us all into jelly, so I go for my heat, see? Well, *that* was a fucking mistake." Corcoran's hand went to his left shoulder, and then he held the bandaged wrist in front of him to illustrate the point.

"My hand is just going inside my coat when the guy in the middle lets fly again. Stands solid right in front of me and just lets this *huge* mother of a foot fly. I tell you, Spence, it felt like a goddamn elephant kicked me. Broke my wrist, see, and the doc says it was lucky it was there because if it hadn't cushioned the blow we might be doing some open heart surgery on me right now.

"Anyway, that puts me out of the action. You know I never could learn to shoot lefty. I sort of stagger back, you know, because a broke wrist is no bed of roses, but I'm trying to keep my eyes open because if I'm going to buy it I want to be there to see it happen. Hurts like a bastard but I'm O.K. I can see anyway. Shit, Spencer, I wish you could of seen..."

"Come on, Joe, come on..."

"O.K. I'm getting there. Well, I'm watching the kid, see, because that's about all I can do, and the three creeps come down on him hard. But he don't move. Spence, he don't move a fucking *inch!* There's an open door behind him and these three Kung Fu creeps in front of him out to kill, and he just sort of stands there staring at them. Real easy like, with his hands up like this, see, and *waits* for them!"

Spencer smiled as he recognized, in spite of Joe's none too precise depiction of it, what must have been the Stance of the Cat-. He nodded. Joe took another drag and blew it out in a cloud.

"Then they came at him. Christ, Spence, I tell you I never seen anything like it in my life. It was better than Dempsey-Tunney. That kid was amazing, just amazing. He lets these three mothers come on him like they all got all the time in the world, and then he whips their asses from here to Frisco Bay.

"They jump him all at once, see, like he's the one they're really after. No shit, they didn't even look at me—they just rush the kid all at once. And his arms, they go out like this, one to each side, and they catch the two bastards on the outside. They're coming in like windmills and he throws them off like they're twigs or something.

"The big guy in the center, he tries a kick again. The kid don't move. Soon as the two outside guys are off, his elbow comes down in front and I hear the big guy's knee go off like a fucking skeet gun. That bastard won't be walking for months, that's for damn sure. Then the other two, they start throwing out legs and arms like it's going out of style. And the kid's just whipping them off like they're so many flies, you know? He moves them back into the center of the room and he just sort of *plays* with them! Spence, I tell you he could of killed the pricks any time he pleased, but he's just out having a high old time, cutting and poking and making them look like a couple of weenies. They can't lay a hand on him! He's dancing around and jumping over the fucking coach and jigging to beat the band. Spence, you ought to of seen that mother's footwork. I swear to God he made Sharkey look like a cripple. I never seen so many moves in my goddamn life!

"It's over pretty soon, I guess. I don't know, I sort of lost track of time. You know, I didn't even notice the pain; here my goddamn wrist is busted and all I can see is this kid doing his thing. That's how good he is, Spence. I wish the hell it could of lasted longer. Just a one-rounder, but what a fucking round!"

He drew on the cigarette again, and his face beamed as if he were the kid who had just caught Hank Aaron's Number 715. Then he wound it up.

"The way he did them in, I'll never forget it. They're throwing hands left and right, see, and all they're getting out of it is black and blue. So they back off, and you can see they got this thing sort of planned out, like they were saying 'If all else fails' you know, we'll try this one. So they sort of split up and try to get the kid between them. And the kid just lays back real easy, lets his hands sort of flop around like he's loosening up, but you can see he's just clowning with them.

"Then it gets blurry, like they all go at the same signal. I mean, these two punks are moving around for position and doing the head-nodding shit with each other so they'll both go at the same time, and the kid—Spence, I swear to God the kid knew *exactly* what they were going to do, and he gets the jump on them! All of a sudden I see these three bodies in the air, like a layer cake. The two punks, they go at him high and low, and I don't know how the hell he did it, but he's laying out flat in the air *between* them—horizontal, see, flat out!—and his foot gets the one of them in the face and his hands come down on the other one's chest and that's it, it's all over. They sort of flop to the floor and the kid, he lands on his feet and puts his hands on his hips and turns to me to see how I am.

"One of them's got a rib cracked, I think, and the other one's got a busted jaw, broken nose, I don't know, the works. The third one, like I say, he can't walk too good...

"He wasted them, Spence. Work of art. He could of nailed them any time, and he just carried them. It's a shame you were out, Spence, I'm telling you, it was the greatest fucking thing I ever seen."

He took a last deep drag on the cigarette and snuffed it.

Spencer squirmed in the bed. "You book them?" he asked.

Joe nodded. "They're in the precinct hospital. You can see them when you get out. Doc says maybe tomorrow."

Spencer grunted. "What do you think of the kid now, Joe?"

Joe shrugged. "Look, maybe it don't mean anything. I don't know about this Kak character, or the Blue Circle, or any of that crap. Maybe the kid's still a nut, I don't know. But I'll tell you one thing sure." Spencer grinned. "What's that?" he asked. "He ain't no punk."

CHAPTER THREE. *THE FACE IN THE MIRROR*

High in the hills above the sleepy little town of Burbank, California, a limber young man with a handsome, faintly Oriental face trudged easily through the loose scrub toward an open space at the top of a rise. There he removed a pair of unusual shoes, arranged the folds of a long pale-blue robe which the easy valley wind had been shifting gently about his body, and sat down. Methodically, with the nearly lackadaisical precision of long custom, he crossed his legs and placed his upturned hands on his knees. He breathed deeply of the close, dry air and then closed his eyes.

Above him the sharp cry of a hawk rang brittle through the quiet of the landscape. The sun had only now begun to send its first faint rays of light over the horizon, and as the young man sat peacefully in the grey of morning, apparently oblivious to the bird's warning, his face gradually turned pink, then ruddy and bright with the dawn. His blue robe moved about him in small ripples, but aside from that the figure which the hawk eyed nervously gave no sign of life, no suggestion of a threat. Soon she satisfied herself that the newcomer meant no harm, and she wheeled majestically away.

Beneath the young man the San Fernando Valley stretched East and West almost to the horizon. The few residents of Burbank who had been jarred awake by the ungentle ministrations of Westclock & Co. were now lolling half-awake, Saturday-woozy, trying to decide whether their plans for an early start to the beach should be overturned by a round of pre-dawn lovemaking or another three hours of slumber. Here and there along the Hollywood Freeway a single automobile spewed the first weekend fumes into the Los Angeles atmosphere, but the narrow strip of pavement that in two hours would be bumper-to-bumper with a million frantic pleasure-seekers had not yet begun to take on the yellow cast that the influx of automobiles had given it all week long, and would impart to it again before noon. The valley looked almost verdant. Not green, to be sure, but not quite fully tarnished either. Dawn at the weekend was still its best hour; before the night lights had gone off and the mist of smog began to rise, the San Fernando Valley had a certain magic timelessness, as if the small and great predations which in fifty years had reduced it from wilderness to wasteland had overnight been abolished. Every Saturday was a reprieve. The arc lamps glittered like lost, land-locked plankton; the few automobiles might have been misplaced from another dimension, so radically did their presence upset and yet, paradoxically, resolve the scene; the sun, streaming down the beige hills toward the West, seemed grandly evanescent, a great antediluvian river come to purge the present of its crimes. It had been this way when the Indians walked these hills, and it would be this way again.

The young man saw none of this. His body reposed in the middle of a small grassy knoll ringed by scrub oak and pine; but his mind was far away.

For the young man whom the hawk had decided to allow free access to her domain was not one of the myriad converts to this or that brand of Oriental mysticism who had begun to populate the hills and canyons of Southern California that fateful autumn of 1963. He was not among those who had recently been "turned on" to Buddha or Krishna or Rama Dabba Du. He was not to be found on the notorious Sunset Strip each Friday night, cadging drinks and enlightenment from passing gurus; nor was his allegiance drawn to any of the many new occultist sects in the area which went by names like The Process and The Gathering and The Thing.

On other hills, in other grassy retreats both East and West of the sleeping town of Burbank, there were perhaps other young men meditating in what might seem outwardly a similar fashion; there were perhaps whole knots of young men and young women devoting themselves at this very hour to the arcane intricacies of recently learned rituals. From Glendale to Pacoima they sat with their faces to the sun.

But the young man on the hill above Burbank was not one of them. He sat in his own circle, and the thoughts which intermittently disturbed and soothed his brain were as far removed in kind and quality from the thoughts of the valley's other "mystics" as the sun in the eye of the hawk was removed from the glitter of chrome below.

For the young man's name was Chong Fei K'ing, and to a very few elect souls throughout the so-called civilized world, he was known as the Master of the Earthly Center.

As the sun began to mix with the smog in the valley beneath him, K'ing's mind floated on the Wind that Blows in the Void.

Beyond life, beyond death, beyond the line that the tortured imagination of the West had placed between them, his spirit soared and plunged, rode the currents of morning and the eddies and trills of a day without beginning and without end. As freely and as mindlessly as the mighty bird of prey above him, flaunting her enormous wingspread theatrically for her own ecstatic joy, his soul caught the rhythm of the thinnest, fairest atmosphere ever conceived by the mind of Man; fully and effortlessly he took the head of the wind, rode it grandly, reckless as doomed youth, open as the virgin's smile, down to the last flicker of brilliance and pain.

Then, out of the mist of eternity, out of the humming of a million spheres, from within a point of piercing light, a sound emerged.

It was a sound that rang like all the rivers in the world, rushing together to drown him. It was a sound like the thunder and like the clacking of electric light that broke the thunder in two. It was a sound at once terrifying and infinitely soothing. Dimly K'ing, or what of K'ing remained to acknowledge and respond, focussed his attention on it, tried to discern the source, the intent, the shape of the sound. A grand cosmic mantra it seemed, more powerful and more devastating than any an earthly guru could relay; it told of the destruction of mighty empires and the death of millions of people, and yet K'ing marvelled, caught half between smiles and tears, that the very sense of overwhelming desolation which the rushing sound carried with it was, in a way even his meditating mind could not fathom, at the same time the source of a tremendous, abiding solace.

He rode with the sound, and he discovered that it did not after all drown him. Did that mean he was worthy of the mightiness? Did it mean he had nothing to fear?

The boy could not say. The man dared not guess. The Master was silent. K'ing rode with the sound, with the flood.

Presently the sound subsided, and K'ing was left as if on the bank of a wild, secluded stream, beaten and bent with the force of the world's waters, yet alive, breathing, awake. About him he seemed to see shards of every civilization that had ever commanded men's allegiance on this earth: the waters, it seemed, had gone back from whence they came—into the earth, into the air, he did not know where—and in their wake they had left a telling message. K'ing sat calmly on the hill. K'ing rose painfully from the dry river bank. The breeze of morning waved his black hair. He looked about him.

The sand was full of gold. Bracelets and earrings and amulets beyond price; vessels of every shape and size; crowns and scepters and tabernacles inlaid with precious stones. All broken beyond repair. The remnants of Atlantis, of the Ninth Dynasty, of El Dorado in a thousand lands, lay strewn about the caked sand of the riverbank, glittering still, mocking, worthless at last. K'ing looked about him, unsure whether to cry or laugh.

For he knew that this was only the surface of it.

For every ounce of gold that lay here abandoned, a pound of flesh had been taken. For every bauble a human life had gone. He was filled with an unutterable sadness, a crisp, biting sense of futility that cut to his heart with a poignancy that the rushing flood had been powerless to evoke. He sat down on the riverbank and his eyes were moist.

Suddenly, above him, he heard the sound of rushing again. But this time the sound was of wings. The beating of wings so large they could encompass the earth, the mighty, deathless ride of a bird that could swallow the world. K'ing looked up. In the air above him, silhouetted against a fiercely burning sun, hovered a huge black bird. A hawk, or a vulture, he could not be sure.

K'ing rose as if in unconscious obeisance and stared at the great shape.

And the creature spoke. It spoke a language that K'ing had never heard before, and yet the boy understood. He listened attentively as the bird told a sorrowful tale of the Indian people who had once inhabited this land: how they had become mighty in war and in wealth, until every living creature from coast to coast had acknowledged them as Masters; how then the power that they had gained eventually proved their undoing. For they had sought to regulate the lives not only of the other men with whom they shared the land, but even of the animals and plants of the earth, whose land it originally had been. When they tried to extend their dominion over the great birds of prey who inhabited the mountain crags, the birds revolted and attacked the people. In one awful night every man, woman and child of the tribe was blinded; their eyes torn out by the vengeful birds of prey. Soon after that the people had disappeared, wandering sightless out into the desert, and were never heard from again.

K'ing could not tell whether the tale was meant as a warning or a threat, but his unasked question was soon answered. With a horrible shriek the bird uttered his name, and then, before K'ing could protest, dropped a glittering object on the sand some yards away from the mystified young man.

Then the bird was gone.

K'ing went to the object, leaned over, picked it up. It was a burnished silver frame, and in the center an oval mirror flashed in the sunshine. K'ing turned the strange object over in his hands and then, as if compelled by a force he did not understand, brought the reflective surface around to face him. What he saw made him drop the heavy object in horror and disgust.

From out of the smoky glass stared a familiar face. It was his face, the face of Chong Fei K'ing. And yet it had no eyes! The eyes had been ripped out, just like the eyes of the unfortunate people of the tale, and in their place stood two hollow bloody sockets. K'ing stared at the reflection in awe, fascinated and repelled at once.

And then a strange thing happened. As he looked into the glass, the blinded face changed shape. The face became fuller, the hair slightly darker, the chin flatter. The mouth twisted into a leering grin, and the eyes, or where the eyes had been, turned into... K'ing could not believe what he was watching, and yet he could not turn from it... the bloody sockets grew in size, distended up and back, changed shape, until they came to be not sockets at all, but the two lurid purplish scars which adorned the evil face of—Kak Nan Tang! Aghast K'ing stared as the evil mouth opened and the voice of his archenemy pronounced a fearful greeting:

"Brother! We are one!"

The glass dropped from K'ing's hands and disappeared into the gentle current of the river. With a start the young Master came out of his trance, as overhead the great wings of the hawk cast an ominous shadow over the grassy knoll where he sat suspended between that faroff country and Burbank, California.

Shaken he got up and walked down the hill.

The young Master of the Earthly Center was too certain of himself and of his mission to be long distracted by something as shadowy as a dream. Yet this dream, this perverse and yet peculiarly enlightening vision, had come to him while he was just emerging from the deepest kind of vision, that which was entrusted to the mystic when his spirit was riding the Wind that Blows in the Void.

45

So K'ing would have had to be dishonest with himself to say that he had not been disturbed by the experience. At the very least it confirmed his suspicion that Kak—and Kak's oddly growing powers—were close by. K'ing was sure of that, the sense of his archenemy's presence had been so strong. At the worst it suggested that Kak's study of Black Magic had actually resulted in his being able to influence events—events in and out of the mind.

No, K'ing did not want to consider that, it was a betrayal of everything Lin Fong had taught him about Black Magic, from the very first days in the Gobi when Kak had expressed an interest in the old man's peachwood box. K'ing thought back with wry amusement of the day months later when he had opened that box to discover the great Master's "secrets" and had found instead only a blank piece of paper.

Yet he knew that Kak still believed in magic, and that he had been practicing it regularly since K'ing had driven him out of the desert. What if... but no, K'ing would not consider it.

Had the vision come from Kak? And if so, what did it mean? It meant that his "brother," as he pleased to call himself, was here in California, and that he was preparing himself for yet another encounter.

K'ing felt it overwhelmingly, a deep and growing sense of foreboding. Never before, in the three years since he had begun trailing his archenemy out of the Gobi, had the sense of Kak's closeness so oppressed and at the same time exhilarated him. It was as if the forces of the cosmos were conspiring with his own appetite to ensure that, this time, Kak would not escape him. The young Master's vision, wherever it had come from and to whatever design, had only served to reinforce his animated frame of mind. He felt now as never before that he and Kak were destined, here in the washed-out, sun-caked hills of southern California, to clash in a combat that would make all their previous encounters seem only contests.

He did not know whether it was the spirit of this bleak and fearful land, so bent toward competition and aggression, that had put him in this frame of mind, or whether something far more shadowy and circumspect—something that fed off the mysterious currents of the universe itself—had compelled him to leave his wife and son behind in New York and seek his fate in furious single combat with Kak in this strange land. But something had pushed or drawn him here, he could not deny it. He felt he was to be tested as never before, and with him, perhaps, the spirit of the land itself.

He did feel more strongly now than ever before the purely personal nature of the fury that lay between him and the Lord of the Earthly Underworld. Mark that up, perhaps, to the rugged individualism of this expansive, xenophobic nation: it was fitting that here in California, last outpost of Westward expansion in the United States, and surely the home of the country's greatest collection of eccentrics, K'ing should be drawn to the fight not as the active agent of something greater than himself, but as K'ing himself, blood rival to the incarnation of earthly Evil. He was, here under the battering August sun, feeling very much himself. It was even, in an unaccustomed but not disturbing manner, a bit of a relief to be alone. He whetted himself for the fight—him and Kak alone. Maybe, he mused with some disenchantment, the face in the mirror had been not entirely wrong: perhaps there was some hidden filial bond between him and the one he had vowed to kill. Perhaps, like the black and white fishes in the emblem of Yin and Yang, they even needed each other. K'ing suddenly shuddered with the recognition of what that might portend: a lifetime of chasing a ghost, of who knew how many more years trying to capture the phantom whose evil presence in the world made life both necessary and intolerable.

It was between the two of them this time. Sun Lee and Sun Tao would be safe in New York with Yussif and The Moor, of that the young Master was sure. For he knew that, like lightning, the Evil of Zedak never struck twice in the same place, but ranged the world round: when once it had scarred a city with its brand of hate, it moved on to fresher fields, new souls to corrupt, new innocents to slaughter. K'ing was gratified that they would be out of danger in New York, and doubly pleased that this meant he would for once have Kak to himself.

But the thought disturbed him nonetheless. Idly he wondered what Lin Fong would have said if he could see his disciple, no matter how reservedly, gloating over the possibility of a personal encounter with his arch rival.

But no, K'ing would not spend time with self-recrimination. He had work to do. And his work was clear: find and destroy the one who had killed his Master.

It was a good season for killing, he thought grimly. Already the hills around Burbank had begun to sprout their harvest of hate; already three mutilated and scarred bodies had popped up, and K'ing knew well enough that Kak would not stop there. In a sense this was Kak's season. Just as Spring belonged to Youdi and Birth and Renewal, Autumn began the dead half of the year, and would, K'ing recognized, be especially attractive as a season for killing to a mind already maddened, already obsessed by cosmic significances, already drenched beyond recall in the murky deliberations of Black Magic.

Dark Harvest. Yes. It would be soon now. K'ing did not know where, or when, or with what arcane pattern this time. But he knew that the New York killings had been a trial run, a prelude to a grim reaping the far-reaching significance of which perhaps not even the twelve Masters of Zhamballah knew.

He pushed open the screen door of the tiny cottage he had rented, walked into the bright kitchen, drew a small cloth patch out of the pocket of his robe, and laid it on the kitchen table. Then he opened the refrigerator door, poured himself a large glass of orange juice, and carried it to the table. He was glad he had chosen to have no servant accompany him to California, for he relished the time he now had entirely to himself, and even the small household tasks that automatically fell to him as a result of his desire for solitude did not bother him. Often, Lin Fong had said, a scrub brush can be as wise a teacher as the sage. K'ing was beginning to understand the old man's meaning.

The patch seemed to glare at him from the table. Against the yellow tablecloth the shape of the black bird showed sable and ominous, and the red characters which K'ing had gone over a thousand times in his mind seemed to shimmer threateningly in the early morning light. Dark Harvest. The time was surely at hand, but what did the characters mean?

K'ing's mind moved to the encounter with the two policemen yesterday. He was glad that Spencer had not been seriously hurt. The man probably did not believe him, but that did not matter. He was an honest man, that was what counted. In time he would see that K'ing was right, and that his apprehension about the havoc Kak could bring to Los Angeles was justified.

He did not doubt that Kak was responsible for the ritualistic killings. His interview with the three hired thugs who had been

48

sent to get him had given him all the information he needed. He had not been at all surprised to learn that the man who had paid them to attack him had been sporting two prominent scars above his eyebrows—and if Spencer and his suspicious comrade needed corroboration for his story, they could get it from the thugs simply by telling them to describe their employer.

And yet there was something wrong in it all. It was not Kak's way. Why should the leader of the most powerful band of Kung Fu fighters in the world—excepting of course K'ing's own allies—hire out a trio of second-rate hit men to take on the one person he certainly knew would not be touched by them? Was it a taunt, a mockery of K'ing's prowess? Was the Lord of the Earthly Underworld merely feeling out the terrain? Was it a test, a warning, or merely sport? K'ing decided tentatively that his archenemy was playing a game of cat and mouse—using the three heavies to keep K'ing's interest in the game while he stored up energy, trained his people...

For Kak to be playing a waiting game, and yet to announce his presence in Los Angeles by such a heavy-handed ruse, pointed to a very dangerous situation. Obviously he wanted K'ing to know he was here—and that in itself was a change of tactics. Had Kak become so confident in his ability to overcome the vengeance at his heels that he could afford actually to *announce* his whereabouts, whereas before he had gone out of his way to conceal them?

And yet he was not showing himself directly...

And then the face in the mirror. Was that from Kak, too? K'ing found himself wondering with a greater apprehension than usual how strong Kak had become since they had last met. He knew the older man was a match for him—indeed, perhaps no two Masters had ever been so perfectly matched—and with Kak holed up somewhere, probably watching his every move, K'ing felt at a distinct disadvantage.

He took it as a sign that a major test was coming. By harvest time he would be fully a Master, or dead.

He knew that Kak knew all this too. In spite of himself, he had to admit that there was a certain perverse bond between himself and the demon he hunted; he knew enough about that demon to suspect many of his thoughts. And he knew that here in Los Angeles, city of angels and city most of all of fallen angels, Kak would soon be coming into his own. He would feel at home in a city

49

surrounded by desert and suffused with a thousand tiny treacheries. He would welcome it. He would bring his deadly legions here in perverse joy, and somewhere in the steel canyons of this sprawling uneasy metropolis, somewhere in the sands of the desert around it, he would be training his fighters for greater and greater battles. He would take nourishment out of the barrenness of this land, and his maimed and tortured soul would grow strong on the little deaths that were its lifeblood.

"Every nut in the country," Spencer had said. Yes, it was a fitting place for Kak to settle in. There was no telling what bleak energies he could extract from this place, no telling what horrid form he could impart to the diffuse, insensate mass of corruption and instability and weakness that made its home here. A true father of chaos he would be if he could, and in no place the two of them had yet been had Kak had so ready a cauldron to brew his evil designs. It was the Devil's own backyard.

K'ing had two questions to answer. One was, where was Kak? That he would have to wait on.

The other was, what purpose had he here? Evil, of course, but of what kind? It was not enough for the young Master to know that Kak had killed here already, and that he would kill again. As in New York, he would have to feel out the pattern to his archenemy's madness, and stop him before it had a chance to run itself out.

K'ing figured that the dancer was all they had to go on, and that while Spencer and his partner were recuperating he would check out the lead they had given him. He had little to lose but time, and that—as long as Kak insisted on remaining hidden—he had plenty of.

CHAPTER FOUR. *WHEN THE VULTURE WAKES*

Donald Blake screamed in agony as the red-hot iron bit into his flesh. Somewhere deep beneath the sands of Death Valley, the young man whom his closest comrades knew as Malachi 7 strained at thick bonds, struggled with the lingering effects of a soporific which had been administered to him a few hours before, and tried to figure out where he was.

His eyes, still heavy with the potion, shot open rapidly as the metal seared his chest again. Just below his right nipple a tiny patch of flesh smoked and stank in the close confines of the cavern. On his left side, between the eighth and ninth rib, a long strip of black skin told where the torturer had placed the first iron, the one that had shocked the young man awake. His nostrils twitched as the acrid smell of his own smouldering body rose to them, and his deep black eyes ranged wildly around the cavern, questioning, pleading, marvelling at what they saw.

He was strapped to a board, hands high above his head, at one end of an underground cave. The board was erect, and he could make out the several figures in the room dimly by the light of four large torches stuck into the walls. Nearest him was a short slender figure whose head was covered by a black hood. The young man who had spent countless hours poring over medieval grimoires recognized the shape of the executioner's mask—except that this mask had an addition, a long curved beak where the breathing hole should be, a vicious silver crescent that danced in the torchlight each time the man moved.

Behind him, along the walls of the cavern, were a dozen other figures, also hooded, although their hoods lacked the silver appendage of the torturer. Silently and immobily they were backed against the ruddy walls of the cave, like monks at prayer or mummies readied for death. Their arms hung dumbly at their sides; they seemed, in the dim light, almost a part of the earthen wall itself.

At the other end of the cave, however, sat a figure whose presence, reclined though he was, commanded a far more acute attention than these. He rested easily in a large earthen throne, his left arm crossed on his left knee, his right hand cupping his chin so that, even in the eerie circumstances, he looked the part of a wayward philosopher contemplating the scene.

51

In the few seconds it took the young man to take this in, the seated figure raised his arm lightly in a signal and, although the man with the iron was still facing his victim, he seemed to understand the unseen command, and laid the glowing poker back in a small brazier next to the board to which Don was secured.

The bound occultist squirmed slightly within the leather straps, breathed a sigh of thanks for the reprieve, and waited to see what the seated figure would do next.

The respite from immediate apprehension allowed him to inspect more closely the lineaments of his host's face. The man was young, Don thought, a good deal younger than himself, and yet his face was lined with the burdens of many years of hardship and frustration. His face had a regal cast, but the owner would not, he could see, be a king any human country might be proud of. This was a man who was used to being obeyed, and one to whom command, rather than government, was the congenial aspect of regnancy. Don saw little kindness in the face, and more than a little cruelty.

It was a flat, rather Eastern face. The thick black hair fell in spiky snatches over a broad, high forehead. The eyes were large, sunken, black, and above them—from the eyebrows to the hairline—the prisoner could make out two purplish scars which seemed to clutch at the face like a claw. His Biblical background brought Cain to mind, and yet Don could feel a more than human wickedness in this place—he knew that, whatever Evil the leader represented, it was sure to be more malignant than that of mere fraternal enmity.

How had he gotten here?

Don remembered:

Last night—or was it this night?—had been Saturday. The meeting had gone well, all was in readiness for the grand feast of the Equinox, to be held four days from now. He had been disappointed in Patricia, for he had hoped she would realize how crucial this time of the year was to the Order. But she *had* sounded really tired, and he had guessed it would not matter if she missed this one meeting (she had been so dutiful these past two years) as long as she was sure to be there on the Equinox. So he had told her it would be all right.

He had gone to the meeting, he remembered, and then gone straight home. That was Sunday morning, wasn't it? Yes, Sunday. Filled with the spirit of the Lords of Light, he had gone to his apartment and set up the apparatus for a private conjuring: the pentangle, the candles and incense, the wand, the magic sword.

He had been practicing, dabbling you might say, in the so-called Black Arts for some time now, partly out of curiosity, partly with the suspicion that there might after all be something in it. That night, Sunday, he had felt so expansive, so complete, so honored by the presence of the supernatural powers which the Gathering had successfully invoked, that he had felt certain that this was the night to begin his study of conjuring in earnest.

So he had set out the materials...

Apparently he had been far more successful than he had intended. What had begun as an ecstatic foray into the world of the supernatural, a grand homage to the lords of creation with whom just then he had been feeling an especial affinity, had ended with him strapped to a board somewhere in a subterranean cavern, quaking before the advance of a third bar of hot metal on his skin.

Were these devils, then? Had he, in his Gathering guise of Malachi 7, actually succeeded in bringing the fallen gods up from the netherworld, only to have them turn on him and subject him to who knew what awful tortures? Don looked fearfully at the brazier, its bed of coals sputtering and hissing in the underground quiet.

He had just finished the initial invocation, he thought...

Yes, that was right. He had not even begun to call down the spirits, but had only purified the circle and invoked the tutelary spirits to guard him from harm. Ironically the Latin came back to him now, here in this unknown cavern from whose baneful designs the invocation had, evidently, been powerless to protect him. In the circumstances the sacred words sounded hollow...

Hue per inane advoco angelos sanctos terrarum, aerisque, marisque et liquidi simul ignis qui me custodiant, joveant, protegant et defendant in hoc circulo.

Then, abruptly, everything had gone white, then black.

A blinding light. So searing, so pure, that the young adept had thought it was the intrusion of the heavenly spheres themselves. And then darkness.

He was now dimly conscious of a throbbing pain at the base of his skull, and it occurred to him that, yes, perhaps he had been struck by something. Perhaps he had been knocked out, attacked even within the sacred circle.

But what powers on heaven or earth could have dared touch him there? And what man or beast could so stealthily have crept up behind him that he had been totally unaware of its presence? The young man moved his head painfully from side to side, as if by this restricted purview of his surroundings he could decipher the riddle of where he was and why he was here.

Malachi 7 was no coward, but he was no fool either, and at the moment he knew he was in trouble. He needed help, comfort. And so he resorted to an ancient device. He prayed. For a moment the Order was forgotten, and the faith of his childhood returned. Slowly and almost imperceptibly his lips began to recite the prayers of his fathers, the old, old songs by which Christians had warded off terror since before Diocletian's armies had begun throwing them in the coals.

Pater noster, qui es in coelis...

His prayer, however, was answered not by legions of angels, but by a single curt command from the ominously regal figure who sat across from him.

"Recant!"

Don's head snapped upward at the sound. A quizzical expression came over his face as his unbelieving ears took in the sound which had presaged torture and an agonizing death for thousands of heretics.

Was he then a heretic? Had the Church found him out, and was this an ecclesiastical trial? His bound limbs shook in spite of their strictures at the thought that he was in the hands not of the infernal powers at all, but of the Inquisition. The awe he had felt at the suspicion that he was in Hell turned to rank terror at the idea that he might only be half-way there and that a series of horrible tortures awaited him before his soul could find release. A lifetime of familiarity with the Bible and with its attendant books, the black magicians' handbooks, Foxe's *Book of Martyrs* and the like, had given him an all-too-vivid notion of what it was like for a suspected heretic, or witch, to fall into the hands of the Church. Burning at the stake was the least of it. That was only the capstone to physical agonies too terrible to speak of...

But now the figure rose, and Don was all but certain that the powerfully-built young Oriental who stood before him majesterially in the firelight was no priest. At least no priest of any Church he had ever heard of. Feebly he opened his lips and begged to utter a question he feared to find an answer for. His voice sounded thin in the cavern.

"Who are you? What do you want of me?"

The figure took two steps toward the strapped victim and raised his arms dramatically toward the ceiling of the cave. Then his cruel mouth opened again and he repeated the command.

"Recant! Recant and submit yourself to the power of the Red Circle—or your body will know the full wrath of Zedak, and of the Chosen of Zedak!"

The unfamiliar names spun dizzily through the half-conscious brain of the captive. He had never heard of the Red Circle, or of Zedak. He had no idea who the bizarre figure was, or what the recantation now demanded of him might entail. Foreswear the Gathering? Was that what the scarred chieftain meant? Was he perhaps the leader of another occultist sect? Had Don been captured as an example to his followers?

Blake was well aware of the blood that had been shed; even recently, in the many small battles that went on daily between the followers of this or that occult pretender in the Los Angeles area. He knew that the one true faith was that of the Gathering, and he believed with all his soul in that faith, but he knew that others were not so fortunate as to have seen the pure white light, and he knew that many of those others bore the Gathering and its members ill will. Dimly he reckoned that the awesome figure he saw before him now, demanding that he recant from some as yet unspecified creed, might well be a member—ho, a leader—of any of those rival sects. And he wondered whether, in this extreme situation, his own hard-won faith would be enough to save him.

Again he cried out silently to the gods he trusted in, the gods that had granted him vision after vision, the gods whose powers extended over heaven and earth.

"Jesus, Satan, Beelzebub, Jahweh," he thought. "Come to your servant's aid."

No answer came. The leader raised his arms still higher and uttered, for the third time, the fearful warning.

"Recant or die!"

Don again tried to speak, but no sound came. He did not know whether it was the failure of his gods to answer his prayer, or his ignorance of what he was being "tried" for in this weird lightless cavern, or the certainty that his captors had no real desire to hear him recant, but his mouth could do nothing but splutter in fear.

For it was clear to him now, as the red-hot iron moved toward his chest again at a second signal from the scarred leader, that he was not going to be given a chance to recant at all: they had him here for their pleasure, and their pleasure had nothing to do with justice or mercy or truth. From the ring of leering faces against the walls of the cavern, their teeth white as grinning skulls beneath the black canopies, he knew that no quarter would be given him. Like a dozen mindless fiends whose only pleasure was the cries of their victims, they opened their mouths and panted in anticipation of his screams.

A third signal from the leader, and the glowing iron struck down at the young man's skin. With a deadly hiss the metal bit through the flesh, and the pungent odor of ritual cauterization filled the space.

Malachi 7 screamed. The dozen leers stretched and relaxed. The torturer thrust the iron again into the coals. Through mist-filled eyes the young Gathering leader saw his unknown tormentor nod his approval.

Now the scarred figure raised his arms again and pronounced the sentence of death.

"Malachi 7, adept of the renegade Order of the Last Reaping, for transgressions both temporal and spiritual against the everlasting and mighty will of the great lord Zedak, and for your refusal to deny your allegiance to earthly powers antagonistic to the will of the mighty Zedak, and for your intemperate persistence in your heretical, fanatic doctrines, I, the Chosen of Zedak and Lord of the Earthly Underworld, pronounce you anathema and declare your life forfeit. Now shall you feel the wrath of the Red Circle! Now shall your body scream under the power of Zedak!"

Barely conscious of what the scarred figure was saying, Don watched the torturer remove the red-hot iron once more from the brazier and bring it toward his skin. This time he raised his eyes to the ceiling of the cavern and prayed only for a speedy delivery from the agony. When the metal hit his skin he choked and gasped, his frame shook with terror, the smell of flesh rose high. Red ran from his mouth where he bit through his lips, ran in long rivulets down his neck, over his shoulders, onto his chest where it mixed with the ash of skin and sputtered on the tip of the poker. The poker cut through the skin toward the boy's heart, and he passed out.

The torturer was still busy, although Don could not see it.

He could not see the searing hot poker describe in his flesh the very characters that the Los Angeles police had found daubed in blood on the nude bodies of Jamie and Melissa Strong. He felt nothing as the iron left its trail of burnt skin, and he could not see the two figures emerge in a gruesome bas-relief from the surface of his sweaty chest: on the left the character for *harvest,* on the right that for *dark.*

Nor could he see a door open, as soon as the gory job was done, behind the scarred leader. He could not see the bare-breasted figure of his favorite female devotee emerge from the shadows and come to stand beside the Oriental leader. He could not see her glazed eyes or her loose mouth or the tiny red circle which had been branded on the inside of her thigh. He could not see her, in a mind-less haze, take the hand of Kak Nan Tang and walk with him the few steps which brought them directly in front of his unconscious body. He could not see Kak place a hood over the girl's head and a long silver sickle in her right hand. He could not see Kak's second nod of approval.

When he awoke a second later, the sound of the scarred leader's voice again filled the cavern.

"Children of America! Minions of the Red Circle! Slaves of Zedak! You are gathered here to witness the sacrifice of an arch pretender to the dominion of Zedak in these Western kingdoms. The wretch you see before you, whimpering for his life, is the once-mighty magician Malachi 7, adept in the renegade and heretical "church" known as the Gathering. He has presumed, through the authority of his office, to challenge the might of Zedak and myself in these regions. Therefore, he must die. For the kingdom of Zedak is absolute, and in this land it shall be known by one name only. A new name I give to you, a new song I sing: the cry of the Vulture shall be heard in the day and in the night! The Cult of the Vulture, long asleep in these valleys, shall rise again from the ashes of the pretender's body. And all things shall be made new.

"When the Vulture wakes, death will rise and dwell among us in majesty! For only in dancing with violent death is a man truly a man!"

57

Almost idly Kak turned to Patricia and raised her right hand in his own. The sickle glittered. Kak released the girl's arm and she continued to hold the blade high. He raised both his arms as well.

"This woman I give to you as Priestess. Once she was indentured to the pretenders of the Gathering. Now the Red Circle has freed her from bondage, and demands as payment for that release that she execute, here and now, the arch pretender who has led her astray from the true path.

"Lilith 3, I give you a new name, and your new name shall be called Wind Woman, for henceforth you will ride on the wind like the Vulture, and strike death down from the skies for the honor and glory of the great lord Zedak!

"Now do I, the Lord of the Earthly Underworld, command you: slay him!"

From behind half-closed eyes, and fighting to remain conscious in spite of a pain that felt like a fire ablaze on his chest, Don tried to focus on the oddly familiar figure that now approached him through the firelight.

He could not know that he was at this moment several hundred feet beneath the surface of Death Valley, California, in a cavern whose egress to the world of Man was in a large limestone rock known as the Devil's Hole. He could not know that the cavern had once been dedicated to the worship of an ancient Apache monster-god known as the Deathbird, or that the few survivors of the Vulture Cult had recently been subsumed under the aegis of Kak's Red Circle. He could not know that the dozen hooded spectators to his death had been, until their recent capture by the Red Circle, the leaders of some of the country's most notorious Satanist sects. He could not know that the young girl now approaching him with an upraised sickle was his former lover Patricia "Boomers" Keele, herself only recently captured by one of Kak's most trusted lieutenants—on the very night, in fact, of the last Gathering meeting.

He only knew what he saw, and he saw a hooded woman with bare pendulous breasts coming step by step nearer to him. A sharp curved object glittered in her right hand. Her eyes, faintly visible through the eye slits of the black hood, were emotionless. She walked as if she were following orders automatically, as if they came from far away.

Her breasts swung slightly in the flickering of the torches, and suddenly Don knew. He knew where he had seen those breasts

58

before. How many times had he caressed them lovingly? How many times had he gently bit them, to hear the slight squeal of pleasure and pain that told him she was ready for him? How many times had he comforted her, held her from crying, assured her that the gifts she had borne and would bear into the world were all that mattered, that no matter what the lusty-eyed men at the dance-hall said or thought, she was a queen...

And now the breasts he had loved were coming toward him again. But the body bore a blade, and the face was blank with drugs, and the woman he had loved was no more. Weakly he opened his mouth in a plea.

"Patty..."

And the sickle flew.

As if she had been trained in the art for centuries by Masters of killing, Patricia Keele brought the gleaming blade down in a long swipe toward the eyes of her lover. The tip of the blade hit a half-inch from the corner of his left eye, and it ripped through the eyeball like a razor, nicking the bridge of the boy's nose as it came out in a shower of blood. In a smooth, unimpeded motion the girl brought the silver crescent up again backhanded, and this time it caught the staring right eye clean in the center, popping it out like a grape onto the floor of the cave.

The young man's mouth opened but again no sound came. A stutter in the back of the throat, a gagging, a quick intake of breath, and the blade came again. This time its heavy tip broke the boy's skull just above the hairline, and the red and silver curve cut through the bone to a brain that was already dead.

Behind the girl Kak Nan Tang dropped his arms.

CHAPTER FIVE. *THE NEW AGE*

K'ing's perfectly disciplined body tensed for action as the roar of a powerful motor came up fast behind him. Without turning he gauged how close the speeding automobile would come, and shifted his stance imperceptibly to the right, his lithe form swaying with the unhurried aplomb that meant survival in the bullring and on the track. His steel-tipped shoe grazed the pokeweed at the side of the mountain road as the small open car skidded an inch from his leg and continued with a screech of tires up around the bend. In a second its motor was a hum in the distance.

K'ing stepped back onto the road. The episode had neither shocked nor unnerved him. The young man who had in his short eighteen years already faced death at the hands of countless assassins was not to be upset by a chance encounter with a reckless driver. He set his face toward the crest of the hill and resumed walking.

It struck him as odd that, here in a landscape almost pristine in its wildness, he had come within an inch of being overrun by a machine. One of those machines that were, by what seemed to him almost conscious intention, destroying the few remnants of wildness that still existed in this strangely acerbic, yet undeniably beautiful land called Southern California. Odd, and at the same time fitting. For, more than any other country he had seen, California was an experiment in contrasts. He could not tell by what unseen organic forces the blatantly disparate elements of this sprawling community were held in balance, and in a perversely comic way he had come to think of Los Angeles—with its rank and noisy communities sitting against a marvellously serene landscape—as America's best image of the Tao. *Concord in dissonance,* he remembered reading somewhere while he was still in the Gobi; here in America, and especially in Los Angeles, the phrase had taken on a special meaning.

As if to add further evidence to his surmise, his foot struck something hard. He looked down. A beer can. Yes, that too was fitting. There was a certain cosmic justice in the fact that the nation which had been blessed with the planet's most extensive range of natural beauty should also be populated by a people maniacally committed to desecrating it. All things pass in time, the young man thought. He did not worry about the beer can.

He did not worry about the beer can, and he did not worry about the car, for he had more important things on his mind this blazing September morning. Almost a week had passed since the disappearance of the dancer who, according to Spencer, was the single lead in the mounting run of slayings.

The single lead to Kak Nan Tang.

K'ing breathed the fresh air of the canyon and smiled grimly in remembrance of the week's events. The fight at the girl's apartment. The talk with Spencer in the hospital. The assurance by the would-be assassins—in *their* hospital, the one at the jail—that it had indeed been Kak behind the attack. Then, the visit two nights ago to the girl's place of employment, the notorious topless club known to its seedy clientele as The Patch.

The Catpatch's owner, a heavy set man dressed from head to toe in maroon—a "jump suit" Spencer had called it—had been noncommittal but in a small way helpful. Yes, Patricia Keele had been employed here. No,,he did not know any of her friends. No, she didn't talk much about herself. But... yes, he did recall one thing she had said about a month ago... struck him kind of funny at the time... he didn't know if it meant anything or not, but...

"'Come September, Mr. G.'—she always called me Mr. G.—T just might be here and gone.' That's what she said. Now I knew damn well she didn't have much bread or else why would she be stripping off for these bozos, so it kind of stuck with me. 'September' she said, like it was a red-letter day or something, like her ship would come in... Help you any, boys?"

Maybe, Spencer had said, and thanks.

September, K'ing thought. It was September now, the real beginning of the fall. Of the harvest season. If Kak were going to strike in L.A., it would most likely be around this time, and the young Blue Circle Master hoped he wasn't hunting geese by suspecting that there was more than a coincidental link between the girl's disappearance, her plans for September, and Kak's obsession with the coming of a dark harvest.

He could do little but wait, however, and hope the harvest might be delayed long enough for him to track down the bloody reaper. Now, he was just "snooping," as Joe Corcoran had called it. Doing a little leg work, checking out the girl's possible haunts. One of her fellow dancers at the Catpatch had mentioned that Patty— "before she got into this occult shit, you know"—used to hang out with a commune somewhere in Laurel Canyon. That was where K'ing was headed now. Follow up every lead, like the cops said. It wasn't very exciting work, but K'ing knew it was necessary, and anyway it was all he could do right now.

And it was good, after all, to be close to the earth again. This short hike up and down the gentle inclines of California's lovely canyons had begun to bring home to him how removed he had been for months—at least physically—from the currents of nature which had been his first and foremost link to the eternal grandeur of the Tao. It was good again to be close to rocks and trees and dirt, good to feel the sun cleanly on his face and hear the sound of thrushes. He relished his early morning meditations on top of the hill behind the small cottage he was renting, and this walk in search of the latest of his archenemy's victims was, in spite of its somber intent, a rare exhilaration for him. He turned his face to the sun and breathed deeply.

He had been winding with the road for perhaps an hour when the scent of sandalwood assailed his nostrils and alerted him to the presence, somewhere in the trees, of others of his own species.

Incense-burners, he thought. It had been a long while since he had sat at the feet of the venerable sage who had been both mother and father to him until he was fifteen, and now the smell of the soft, aromatic wood brought those days back to him with a calm, titillating poignancy. He could see the old man dropping an extra pinch of amber powder on the coals, and the thin beige smoke curl toward the sun. He could see the old man's kind, wise eyes close as his spirit sought the Wind that Blows in the Void.

And he could see the inquisitive, skeptical face of a boy two years older than himself—the as yet un-scarred face of his fellow pupil, his playmate, his brother in arms. The face of Kak Nan Tang.

The vision upset him. He shook it off and directed his attention to the trees, from where the sandalwood scent had come. He left the road and plunged in. A hundred yards into the trees a high wall of sumac and oak confronted him. He trudged through it and found himself at the edge of a small clearing, in the middle of which a circle of five men and women sat around a wood fire. Behind them the white walls of a long canvas tent caught the sun brightly, and in front of the rustic dwelling K'ing could see an infant's cradle, rocked easily by the hand of the young man nearest to it. He approached slowly, and was met halfway across the clearing by a handsome woman of about forty, who had risen from the circle as soon as he had broken through the brush. Her voice was gentle and her eyes smiled.

"Welcome, Brother. Will you eat with us?"

K'ing nodded his thanks politely, and joined the five around the fire.

The woman introduced the company as the New Age Commune, then asked what they might call him.

"My name is Chong Fei K'ing."

"You are welcome," said the woman.

She passed him a plate full of greens, nuts, and roots, and again K'ing was reminded of the desert where he had come to manhood. Again he saw the aged Master who had taught him almost everything he knew, bent over a dish of simple food given to him by the nomads thankful for his constant vigilance.

The meal was tasty and filling. They ate in silence, and this afforded K'ing the opportunity to inspect the members of the little company. The woman who was apparently its leader was grey and tanned, and her eyes sparkled with a hidden mirth that might have done justice to a much younger woman. The rest of the group were younger—in their twenties, K'ing guessed. Two men and two women. One of the men had a full black beard and the other was clean-shaven; one of the women wore nothing above her waist, the other, like the older woman, wore a simple muslin shift. They smiled at him without embarrassment or concern, and K'ing was pleased to discover that even in this overtly aggressive country there were still pockets of life where men and women were content to let each other be.

When the meal was done one of the young men cleared the plates, which he brought to a basin near the tent. Then he returned with a bowl of chokecherries, which he set in the center of the circle. K'ing had just helped himself to a handful of the juicy fruit, and was about to test the obviously rigid protocol of the group by inquiring whether any of them had ever heard of Patricia Keele, when the grey-haired woman turned amiably toward him and extended her left hand toward the two young women across the circle.

"It is our custom, Chong Fei K'ing, to make our guests feel truly welcome. If my daughters please you..."

The implication was unmistakable, and yet K'ing did not know what to say. He was, needless to say, not accustomed to being offered the sexual favors of attractive young women whom he had met only moments before. He knew his fidelity to Sun Lee was so firm that he would not even entertain the notion of accepting the woman's offer, and yet he did not wish to offend this pleasant company by mocking its customs.

He looked at each of the young girls in turn. Each was striking in her own way, and the young Master had to admit that at this moment the most intense concentration on the truth and meaning of the Tao was needed to dispel from his mind the unusually strong temptations that were now making their presence felt there. But the thought of Sun Lee's beautiful, pliant body sustained him, and he answered slowly, with careful deliberation.

"I am not of your country, and I am not entirely familiar with your customs. I am honored that you see fit to offer me your daughters, and I can see that they must rightfully bring pride to a mother's heart. Yet I hope you will forgive me for refusing, for what you suggest I could not in good conscience submit to without forsaking my own custom."

He hoped the speech, formal as he knew it was, had not sounded presumptuous. He looked anxiously at the older woman, but she only smiled and nodded her agreement.

"As you wish," she said.

They ate the chokecherries. He was pleased that the girls did not seem dejected by his refusal, and that they still regarded him with the polite curiosity which had pervaded the entire meal.

After a few moments one of them spoke.

"Your eyes say that you are not at ease with yourself, Chong Fei K'ing, although your tongue is eloquent. Why have you come here?"

The young Master was pleasantly surprised. It was not often that someone outside his immediate circle of fellow Taoists—Sun Lee and The Moor and Yussif—saw into his heart. He found it easy to keep his eyes off the young woman's taut, tanned breasts, because her open, friendly gaze was so commanding in its obvious simplicity. He grinned in spite of himself.

"I am, as I have said, not of your country. I do not know what your Way is here in this canyon, but I have been told that many of the members of the communes in this area know each other, and I am seeking someone who was, I am told, once a member of one of them. More recently she has been a member of a group called the Gathering. Her name is Patricia Keele."

There was a moment's silence, and then the bearded young man spoke. "I knew Patty Keele a while ago. I had not heard that she had joined the Gathering, and I am sorry to hear it. Yes, she once lived with friends of ours over in Topanga, but she left the canyon a couple of months ago to go to North Hollywood, I think. We haven't seen her around here since then. Why do you want to find her?"

The small commune listened attentively as K'ing related, for the second time in a week, the salient details of his quest for Kak, and finished the story by confessing his suspicions that the missing girl was in the hands of his arch-rival. This time, he was pleased to see, his audience showed more respect, even a tinge of awe, for the tale. It was not that the policemen's skepticism had upset him, or that he needed the reassurance that polite attention afforded, but it was nice for a change to be among people who could afford to think the best rather than the worst of a stranger.

"Quite a story," the older woman said when he had finished. Then she turned to the young man who had spoken earlier. "Now, what about this Gathering?"

"Well, I'd call them fanatic millenarians," he began. "They take Biblical names and they believe that the Second Coming is at hand. They also practice Black Magic and they apparently think that Jesus and Satan are only two names for the same person. I don't know if they're crazy or just confused, but I know that Patty—you remember how lost she was when she came here, how much she wanted somebody to give her an answer?—would be a likely target for their recruiting."

He turned to K'ing. "She was in and out of every fad in the canyon when she was here: health foods, sex therapy, acid, acupuncture, T'ai Chi, you name it. I hadn't heard that she got hooked up with the Order, but it wouldn't surprise me. Come to think of it, wasn't she hanging out with that Don Blake character— the writer who was doing all those occult mysteries?"

The question was directed at the girl to his left. She nodded. "And I know *he* would be linked up with the Order, if anybody would," she said.

"You mention the Order," said K'ing. "Is this the same thing as the Gathering?"

"Yes," replied the bearded man. "The official name of the Gathering is, I think, the Order of the Last Reaping. Like I say, they're millenarians, so they're always ready for the last judgment and so on. Their big season is right now, in fact—autumn, you know. Seems to me that they hold their big service on the Witches' Sabbath..."

"Which would be when?" K'ing's voice betrayed a slight agitation.

"Oh, very soon. Last week in September. The Autumn Equinox, in fact. It varies from year to year, but it's always around harvest time. Hence the last reaping."

K'ing nodded. The older woman spoke quietly. "Is this the information you wanted?"

"Yes," said the young Master. "More, in fact, then I really wanted."

At the invitation of the commune members K'ing spent the night with them. After a light and delicious rabbit stew, served on a bed of plantain, the group retired early into the tent which served them all as a communal quarters. The bearded young man, whose name, it turned out, was Rich, elected to stay up and talk with the newcomer about the New Age they were all patiently awaiting.

"It will be a time of peace and plenty," he began with a touch of somber reverence in his voice. "Once again the fields will be filled with game, and the predations of men bent on money and madness will be at an end. The people will live on the land and be nurtured by the land—by the wind and the rain and the sun. The cities will soon have outlived their usefulness, and they will be abandoned, and with them men and women will abandon the false values and petty hypocrisies on which the cities stand. Then they will join us, and return to the earth which is our common mother. After two centuries of betrayal, the simple ways of the red men we exterminated will again take precedence, and the voice of the turtle will be heard in the land."

"Do you believe, then," asked K'ing, "that you are the vanguard of a larger movement?"

The young man's voice lost some of its reverential hush as he labored to describe to K'ing the full meaning of their project.

"No doubt of it. We believe that we are only the first of many who will recognize that the days of the urban world are numbered, and that the only hope for man's survival lies back in the fields where he began. Already, throughout California and as far North as Oregon, young people are leaving their families and jobs and getting together again in a simpler, more healthy way of life. They are coming to understand that the Indian's way was the right way after all, that this country was not meant to support factories and ugly cities, but to remain as rich in natural harmony as it was when the first Europeans came here. The Europeans destroyed this country, and their children's children are now turning their backs on Europe and European ways, and trying—just like the first settlers tried—to make a new life in the New World. *Really* new, you know, because it will be based on new values: on love and harmony and frankness, on amity among all peoples. 'And all things will be made new,' the prophet said. We believe that, and we're doing something about it."

"But will you be able to escape the world for long, the world out there—will it not press in on you, and destroy what you have started?"

"There is a danger of that, I confess. But we believe that we can resist their blandishments *and* their threats. We believe that in the end they will have to see that our way is the right way, or they will die. We cannot force them to be free, that is true, but we can set an example, and that is what we are doing here. It's working," he finished simply.

"It is working here, in this small circle. But in the greater circles of the world outside, men are still governed by the same sad designs that have governed them for many ages—even in the time of the Indians. Do you not think so?"

"In the time of the Indians?" Rich's voice was incredulous.

"Yes. Were there not wicked men among the ancient tribes, as well as good ones? Were there not sorcerers and those who practiced Black Magic and war lords who lusted only for the pleasure of battle—just as there are today? Were there not battles and deceptions and killings and rapes and lootings among the Indians, just as among other people?"

K'ing's voice was strained, and it was evident that it was as painful for him to suggest this possibility as it was for Rich to hear it.

The face of the young communard clouded briefly, then relaxed. "What you say is true. There is an ancient legend about a huge battle between the Thunderbird god and a new, wicked god who called himself the Vulture. The battle was supposed to take place a very long time ago. It was said that before the battle there was peace and prosperity in the land; no one went hungry, no one looked in envy at his neighbor, fighting was unheard of.

"After the battle, although the Thunderbird won, there was a new spirit in the land. No one could say how it had come about, and no one could abolish it. The new spirit was the spirit of hatred, of evil, and it was the legacy of the Vulture god to the land which had refused him sanction. For centuries after that, the power of the Vulture, though subdued throughout the centuries by the tribes' allegiance to the Thunderbird, was never far distant from the lives of the people. Whenever a child died prematurely, whenever, a man struck his neighbor, whenever a shaman deceived the people, they would say it was the work of the Vulture. His power is still felt today. Perhaps it is felt most of all in the cities of this land. Yes, there the bird of death is very strong."

He paused for a moment, looking into the flames of the dying fire as if seeking the answer to an overwhelming question, and then went on.

"It is curious that you should ask this question now, at this season. I said this afternoon that the members of the Order of the Last Reaping held their high feasts on the Witches' Sabbath, at the Autumn Equinox. Well, that—or so the legend goes—was true of the cult which worshipped the Vulture as well. Perhaps this is a coincidence and perhaps not I would hate to think that there is any connection between them.

"No," he finished hurriedly, as if trying to convince himself of something he did not really believe, "the Vulture Cult has been dead for many years."

"For good?"

Rich's face darkened again. "I hope so. We believe, you see, that there is such a thing as progress, that human existence moves toward an inexorable, benevolent conclusion. We believe that the beast has been buried, and that the New Age dawns. I know that you are a Taoist, and that such a notion must be repugnant to you..."

K'ing smiled. "Not repugnant, surely. My idea of an earthly paradise is perhaps different from yours, and it, is called by another name, but the idea is not » repugnant."

"A little difficult to fit in with the classical Taoist idea of conflict as a sustaining principle of the universe, isn't it?"

"Perhaps," conceded K'ing. He could see that the young man, whatever his predilections for fanciful sanguinity, had at least done some thinking. "I meant only that it is dangerous to suppose we can get rid of evil by ignoring it, or even by living well ourselves. Sometimes we must fight it, do you not think?"

"And kill for Christ, you mean?"

K'ing caught the barb neatly, without flinching. "If a man means to burn my house, I must prevent him or I will soon be without a house."

"If a man means to burn your house, it's a good bet it's because he has no house of his own. Give him one, then—look around, there is plenty of space to go around—and he will have no need to burn yours in spite."

"Sometimes," K'ing replied painfully, "men do evil without knowing that they are doing it. And sometimes they do evil knowing they are doing it, but it pains them to realize it. But sometimes they do evil knowing full well that they are doing it, and it actually brings them pleasure. It is the last kind of man I am speaking of."

"I have not met any men of that type," said Rich.

K'ing's face clouded. "I have."

The two young men stared into the fire for several minutes. Finally K'ing spoke. "I do not believe that your way can lead to the new age you speak of, but if I did believe it I would work with all my will to, help you. At least I can offer you my thanks for your friendship and hospitality, and say this: may each of us find his own way."

Rich's face gleamed in the firelight. "Thank you, brother. Amen to that. Perhaps if you believe in a thing hard enough, then— whatever the course of human history is doing—it comes to pass."

If you believed in a thing hard enough. K'ing thought of Zhamballah, and of his place as Master of the Earthly Center. What was Zhamballah, and where? Did he believe in it strongly enough to make it come to pass?

"Perhaps," he said.

70

K'ing had been asleep about an hour when a small noise awakened him with a start. He sensed danger, and his finely-tuned body sprang up, ready for action.

His eyes scanned the floor of the tent. One body was missing. Rich's. Quietly, so as not to wake the other sleepers, the young Master rose and crawled through the flap of the tent.

The moon was almost full, and at the far edge of the clearing K'ing could see his new friend peering into the brush. He seemed agitated, nervous, even (if such a word could be used in this peaceful compound) a bit apprehensive. K'ing began to walk toward him, and was about to call out to him when he heard Rich call out instead.

"Who's there?"

Before K'ing eyes saw the attacker some acute internal sensor had registered his presence. No leaf had moved, no noise had disturbed the silence of the woodland night, but the young Master's heels dug into the grass of the clearing and his mouth opened in a shout of warning.

"Duck, Rich!"

Instinctively Rich dropped to his knees, and at the same instant a slim black shape hurtled out of the bushes behind him, its deadly heels seeking a target in the young man's skull. K'ing's shout had been enough to save his friend's life, but not enough to save him from a fearful gash on the temple as the attacker's steel-tipped shoe laced his skin. He fell to the ground stunned, his blood staining the grass.

K'ing was at his side in a second, his own deadly shoes darting out fiercely at the black-clothed figure before him. The attacker weaved masterfully and was on his feet, five feet away, before K'ing had time to follow through. K'ing's eyes glinted with excitement as he realized that Kak had finally sent him a worthy opponent.

The two Kung-Fu fighters circled slowly, and K'ing's glance went from the man's hooded head down his long angular body, and back to the silver object mat lay suspended on the black sweater before him. He had no time to inspect it now. He had no time for thought at all.

They closed.

K'ing shot a Ram's Head at the black figure's head, and turned it immediately into a Whipping Branch Party as the figure dodged the attack and came at him with a Hammer Blow. The man's right hand clenched into an answering Ram's Head and darted toward K'ing's exposed chest. K'ing swivelled and swept a Pounding Wave inches past the man's nose, then backstepped quickly as the man's Knife Point slashed up within an inch of his throat.

He came back with a barrage of Hammer Blows. His opponent blocked them well, circling all the while to place K'ing's back toward the smouldering fire.

The Blue Circle Master saw what the hooded figure intended to do, and braced himself for the Elephant Kick he knew would come any instant now. He kept up the thundering attack above while his mind concentrated on positioning himself to deflect the powerful kick when it came.

The figure's parries were powerful, more like attacks than defenses. He had very thick arms, and K'ing's wrists were beginning to ache with the repeated crash of bone against bone. He dropped back a foot and came back at once with a savage Knife Point that left a trail of red just above the man's left ear. K'ing's fake had been so expertly timed that the man's defensive Whipping Branch had come an instant too soon, and left his face open for the deadly jab. Had he wanted to, K'ing could have finished him with a blow to the throat, but he wanted this one alive if possible, because he knew that that was his only real chance of finding Kak. So he had gone for the ear, and now blood trickled down the man's cheek.

The blow had thrown him temporarily off guard, and now K'ing had the advantage. Another Ram's Head flew toward the man's skull, and a Swooping Bird knocked it aside. A faked Monkey Blow turned into the darting tail of the Scorpion, and the crack of his knuckle on the man's wrist told K'ing he had got the bone.

Now he backstepped slightly, and his opponent followed in a rush of Pounding Waves. K'ing knocked each one in the air in turn, his Whipping Branches flying like twigs in a hurricane. In a second his back was again to the fire, and again he braced himself. This time the man took the bait, and let the heavy front kick go directly toward K'ing's crotch.

K'ing swivelled in that same almost imperceptible motion that had saved him from the car this afternoon, and brought his elbow down in a fierce Monkey Blow toward the man's exposed knee. He meant to cripple his opponent rather than kill him, and a crushed kneecap would be the quickest way.

But inches before he connected, the man did something that convinced K'ing, if by this time he still needed convincing, that the hooded figure was indeed an emissary from the Lord of the Earthly Underworld.

It was a move so daring in its deceptive simplicity that K'ing knew the man could have learned it only from a very great Master. Still balanced on his left foot alone, he withdrew his extended right leg just long enough to allow K'ing's Monkey Blow to pass harmlessly by, and then shot it out again, this time pointing the steel-tipped toe so that the Elephant Kick became a searing Lightning Kick.

It was a move, as Lin Fong had often told him, that only two kinds of fighters would use: very good ones and very bad ones. It was evident to K'ing by now that this strange figure belonged in the former category.

The young Master's own lightning reflexes moved him far enough back, in the split second he had, so that the vicious kick penetrated no more than a fraction of an inch into his thigh.

It was not a serious wound, but the man knew he had drawn blood, and it gave him new courage. Now he descended on K'ing with Lightning Kick after Lightning Kick. K'ing stepped nimbly around them, an artful dancer amid a sea of knives.

They continued to circle, and now, in the corner of his eye, K'ing could see that the other members of the commune had been awakened by the noise, and were standing, astonished, before the tent. Each time one of the fighters attacked a hush would seem to rise palpably from the small knot of communards, as if in shocked recognition that, inexplicably, the evil of the outside world had intruded into their sylvan paradise. Over the shoulders of the dancing black figure K'ing spotted Rich's grieved and bloodied face among those of his friends.

The attacker struck again, this time daring a Dragon Stamp. K'ing dodged it easily and replied with a Lightning Kick that caught the swaying figure cleanly in the hip. He tottered slightly and jumped back out of the reach of K'ing's deadly shoes. K'ing could tell he was tired, and he reasoned that, even though the man had been superbly trained, he probably had had little enough practice against real Masters.

Now the man moved slowly to his right, closer to the glowing heap of coals which were all that remained of the fire. He was trying, it seemed, to keep his distance from K'ing; he delivered a series of short, erratic Dragon Stamps which kept the young Master just out of his way. K'ing tried a Knife Slash and then another Scorpion Blow, but the first barely grazed the figure's shoulder, and the second fell short by several inches. His opponent skipped lightly back and again to his right.

Suddenly the man jumped a full foot to his right, and he was directly across the fire site from K'ing. K'ing could see his chest rise and fall evenly with a deep breath of reprieve, and then the man stopped moving.

Stolidly he planted himself in the earth ten feet from K'ing, and glared menacingly across the glowing coals. The silver object flashed in the dull light as the black-clad figure gradually raised his hands in the Stance of the Cat.

And now K'ing could see what the object was. Against the black background of the man's turtle-neck it swayed evenly, like a hypnotist's charm, and K'ing found himself gazing at it in rapt attention, almost for the moment forgetting the situation and the danger to his new-found friends.

It was curved and sharp, and it glowed now with an unnatural light as if illuminated not by the glow of the coals, but from within.

It was a talon. The talon of a huge bird of prey. Of a hawk or a falcon.

Or a vulture.

The hooded figure stood still on the other side of the fire, and to his horror K'ing found himself oddly drawn to the glittering object on his chest. It seemed to pulse in the night, to contract and expand like a thing alive. K'ing could not keep his eyes from it. As he stared, fascinated by a power he did not understand, his opponent gradually dropped his arms to his sides, then slowly began to raise them again in a kind of salute. Amazed and immobile the boy watched as the hooded figure brought them up, straight out, then high above his head.

The mouth beneath the mask opened and K'ing heard for the first time the ritual greeting of the Vulture Cult. The man spoke

74

in a language he did not understand, and yet K'ing was sure he had heard it before.

Yes. It was. It was familiar. The man was addressing him as "Brother" and K'ing now began, to his horror, to understand the words.

It was the language of the vision! The arcane tongue in which the huge bird had addressed him on the banks of the dessicated stream. Its sonorous, fateful tones sang, brittle and cold, across the fire.

"When the Vulture wakes..." the voice began.

K'ing tried to move. He tried to call up the strength to leap across the endless chasm between him and the assassin, to come down screaming at his throat...

But he could not move.

It was as if the hooded figure were in fact a hypnotist and had commanded him to be still until the invocation was done. K'ing's limbs would not obey the urgings of his mind, and the glittering talon blinded him.

Then, from somewhere beyond life and beyond death, came the answer. It was as if a fog had lifted and K'ing saw clearly for the first time in days. He saw what Kak had been trying to do to him. He understood why his arch-enemy had kept himself hidden, storing up vital energy for the coming battle, while his lackeys worked on K'ing's mind. Now he found the one word, the one countering sign, that could dispel all the mists and madnesses of the Red Circle, all the strange obfuscatory devices of its minions, all the captive power of its slaves.

His mouth opened. Stiffly and painfully he fought against the charm that lured him to his death across the circle. Slowly the lips parted and from the depths of his soul his spirit cried for release.

"Zhamballah!"

Instantly the hooded figure's words became garbled, instantly K'ing was deaf to their sound. The man spoke gibberish, looked lamely about the circle of onlookers, dropped his arms. Then, in a motion so swift that none but K'ing saw it, he reached to the hanging talon, withdrew something from it, threw it into the coals.

Redder than blood, brighter than moonlight, flames shot to the top of the clearing. And K'ing heard, this time fully awake, the sound of a thousand rivers.

He leaped.

His body became the body of a raging cat, and his right hand tightened into the form that had scarred Kak Nan Tang for life: the form of the K'ing Tiger Claw.

Through the column of fire the Master flew, and his hand raked out savagely, seeking his tormentor's eyes.

But the man was gone.

His flight had been so swift that none of the anxious communards had seen him move, and not a branch swayed to mark the path of his escape. The woods were silent, and the fire died down behind K'ing.

He looked quizzically at his hand. In it was the heavy, burnished pendant, locked like the hand itself in the shape of a claw. K'ing stared at it without speaking.

He had no idea how long he stood there. Time seemed to stop until the frightened voice of one of the young girls startled him to attention.

"Come here, quick!"

K'ing followed the others to the edge of the clearing, to the spot where the hooded figure had first sailed into sight. The girl was kneeling on the ground, bent over something.

A body.

K'ing inspected the face dispassionately, beyond shock now, and nodded grimly as he recognized, for the second time in a week, the work of the Red Circle.

The body was that of a young man. Its bare chest was branded with the Chinese characters for *dark harvest,* and its eyes had been ripped out by a sharp object. The head was caved in just above the hairline, and blood drenched the once-handsome face.

The girl who had found the body whimpered softly and turned to fall into the arms of the woman who called her daughter. Her companions looked briefly at the mutilated corpse, winced, and turned away.

Only Rich hesitated before the gory sight. He knelt solemnly and peered closely at the battered head, as if trying to assure himself of something. Then he raised himself up and looked at K'ing, tears glittering in his eyes.

"It's Don Blake," he said.

CHAPTER SIX. *THE STRIP*

"Goddamn crackpots!"

Joe Corcoran's voice was sharp, biting. His eyes glared at K'ing as if the epithet were meant to include him, but the young Master only looked evenly back at him, a slight smile turning the comers of his mouth.

He was not impatient with this brash, suspicious man: nothing, he knew, was to be gained by impatience. He sat calmly and waited for Corcoran's indignance to play itself out. He was a little sorry that Spencer had not been here when he arrived, for he had wished simply to deliver his message to the calmer, older man, and get back on Kak's trail. He had not expected to find Corcoran, fuming over a copy of the L.A. *Times,* whose front page carried the story, replete with photographs, of Donald Blake's murder. He had not expected to have to contend with the intemperance of this nervous cop, or to have to sit still for his veiled accusations.

But he was not impatient. He had seen Joe's type before, seen them burn up in their own thwarted energies. They did not bother him. He sat quietly and waited for Spencer. His partner's voice rose and fell erratically.

"I can't understand it. These kids got everything they need, and then they go out and blow it on this crap. Satan sects! What a lot of malarkey. Take this kid here, he probably comes from a good home, nice parents, went to college and all. All the advantages, you know? And what does he do with it? Gets himself gussied up in black tights. Gets tied up with these bums. Gets himself killed.

"Serves him fucking right. Why the hell wasn't he out working? They're plenty of goddamn jobs out there. Just like those goddamn hippies over in the canyon, sitting around on their asses, screwing and blowing their minds all day long—what the hell good are they?"

He picked up the paper and rustled it as if the rearrangement would make the whole sordid business clear. Then his tone mellowed.

"Hell... I don't know. You can't tell folks how to live, I guess. They got to go out and make their own mistakes." He stared at the cover picture, frowning. "Kid can't have been more than twenty-five. What a fucking waste."

K'ing was silent, respectful of the limited grief that the man was willing to allow himself in his presence. He waited.

Joe struck a match and lit a cigarette, then turned his attention to K'ing.

"All right," he said. "What can we do for you today?"

"Perhaps," K'ing said, "we can do something for each other. I have come about that." He indicated the paper.

"This?" Corcoran was suddenly all business. "What do you know about this?"

"You know from the story that the body was found a hundred yards from the main road up Laurel Canyon. I happened to be there at the time. As a guest of the people who discovered the body."

The young Master reached in to his pocket and laid the silver talon on Corcoran's desk. "The young man's murderer left this. I wonder if it may be of some help."

Corcoran picked up the heavy object and turned it over in his large hands. Then he laid it back on the desk and eyed K'ing closely.

"You say you was staying in the Canyon last night?"

"That is right."

Corcoran shifted in his seat, and K'ing could see he was working up to something. Deliberately the policeman leaned forward, spoke crisply.

"I would like to know what the hell you were doing there. How come you happened to be there just when the body was discovered? You didn't by any chance have nothing to do with this kid becoming a corpse, now, did you?"

K'ing said nothing, and in the silence the two could hear the click of a lock as Ben Spencer, a bandage around his head, closed the door behind him. Joe's head snapped left, and King's turned slowly to the right, nodding a respectful welcome.

"Take it easy on the kid, Joe. I been standing here, and I heard what he told you. It's true. He was just a guest. Didn't have any part in killing the kid. What he didn't tell you is that he tore ass out of the creep who actually *did* burn the guy. So set your mind at rest. This kid"—Spencer's voice was affectionately respectful, and K'ing had a momentary impression that he was going to lay a fatherly hand on his shoulder—"risked his life protecting Ma

Garvey and her little brood from an attack from some Kung Fu creep with a hood over his head. Ain't that right, Mr. K'ing?"

K'ing nodded bashfully.

"And Ma," Spencer went on, "corroborates his story exactly. Lay off him, Joe. You ought to be putting him in for a citation."

Corcoran's face held an odd expression of bemused incomprehension. It was tinged, K'ing thought, with some anxiety. The man turned to him again, nodded with some embarrassment, mumbled an apology, and excused himself from the room.

K'ing's eyes followed him curiously as he went out the door, then they shifted to Spencer and sought an explanation.

The older detective smiled. "Joe's a little short on the amenities, but he's a good man, you can believe that. Only right for him to be suspicious, too. But you just put him in your pocket, though it might not look like it.

"You see, Joe put in a special request to join this squad a few years back after his brother was done in by a creep they called the Tarot Murderer. Joe comes from a pretty strange family, all in all—he's what you might call the one white sheep of the family. All his brothers and sisters are astrologers, poets, circus people, herbalists, you name it. Joe just didn't fit, and I guess he joined this detail to try and understand them. Or to keep them out of hot water if he could.

"Anyway, an older brother and sister started a commune out in the hills a few years back. They were just getting started when the brother was bumped off by the Tarot guy. Really tore Joe up. That's when he came here. Vowed to get the bastard, but he seems to have gone underground, at least for the time being.

"Well, Joe's sister carried on. Became a pacifist, I think, in a kind of eccentric retaliation. Married a preacher name of Garvey. When he died she moved out to the Canyon, started preaching herself. About the New Age."

Spencer raised an eyebrow and K'ing nodded with grim amusement. It was obvious to the policeman that the young Master did not have to be told who Corcoran's sister was.

"Joe'll be grateful to you now, son, and that's a good man to have on your side, believe me."

K'ing said nothing. He tilted his head slightly, and Spencer's eyes went to the desk. The silver talon gleamed cruelly on top of the picture of Blake's body. He leaned over and picked it up. A low hum started back in his throat.

"You have seen one like it before?"

Spencer nodded. "This come from the guy in the hood?"

"Yes," said K'ing simply.

"Yeah, I've seen these before. On the Strip. There's a little occultist shop called Abraxas. Used to be a great burger joint, I don't know why the hell they tore it down. Guy who works there, real nervous type, I think I saw him with one of these a few months ago. Some kind of amulet, but I don't know what group it belongs to."

"Does the Order of the Last Reaping ring a bell?" asked K'ing.

"Don Blake's crew? Yeah. But they don't go in for this kind of thing. Too vicious for them. In spite of all their blarney, they're really just a bunch of kids toying around with magic. Don't think they'd get into talons. Looks too much like a weapon, you know? Could really rip you up."

K'ing waited until the significance of what he had said dawned on Spencer. It took only a second. He looked from the talon to the picture of Blake's shredded face and back again. Then he grinned at K'ing.

"Could be," he said. "You want to check it out?"

"Of course. And quickly. I have reason to believe that whoever is behind the murders is working up to a grand finale on the Autumn Equinox. That's in three days."

"All right," said Spencer. "Tell you what we'll do. I'll run down the list of remaining Order people and grill them. You take the Strip. It's really more of a lark than station-house questioning, but I'm poison down there, and if I came with you we wouldn't have a prayer of getting any nearer to our friend—whoever he is."

K'ing smiled at the omission of the name, pocketed the talon, and rose to go.

"By the way," said Spencer. "You got any idea who you're after?"

"I have an idea," said K'ing.

Lieutenant Joseph Corcoran was not the only one who had been upset by the murder of Malachi 7. Along the mile-long ribbon of asphalt known as the Sunset Strip, every petty occultist, palm-reader, clairvoyant, and fundamentalist millenarian who had ever heard of the Gathering now walked in fear and trembling.

K'ing had seen fear before. He had been so close to it he could smell the dry, musky stench of it, and although he had not yet learned to feel it himself, he knew when it was near him. He felt it on this garish street, felt it settle like a cloak.

It was in the twittering laughter of a teenage girl, responding just a little too warmly to the stale jokes of her blind date. It was in the effusive apologies of leather-jacketed rowdies who bumped him on the pavement. It was in the harsh riposte of a waiter whose customer had just asked for extra onions. It was in every tilting head and blinking eye and every ear that tried to deafen itself against the rumbling and squeaking all around it.

Earthquake weather, the Californians called it. When the madness crept up slow from the earth itself, wound around your ankles in a silent, invisible net, made you trip and right yourself in your mind's eye a thousand times a block.

The strollers were different tonight. To K'ing the difference was not apparent, for he had never before walked that mile of seductive neon barbarism that the locals called "the Strip." But it was there, as subtle and as palpable as mist.

His eyes took in the scene as his mind searched for the name Abraxas.

Two young girls with taut upthrusted breasts that showed clearly through the gauze of their blouses passed him giggling, caught in the delicious throes of drug-induced illusion. Behind them a boy with a shaven head and a single gold earring tried as inconspicuously as possible to catch sight of what, if anything, they were wearing under their thin, wind-tossed skirts. Passing K'ing he caught the young Master's eye and hurriedly averted his own.

Lounging against the sides of buildings were whores of every color, age, sex, and physical description. Huge black women with blond wigs; buxom corn-fed lasses just in from Ohio, selling their bodies for dinner or drugs; a little redheaded boy who looked like a shoeshine kid, bulging at the belt from a padded basket; a tiny Mexican girl no bigger than Sun Lee, the straps of her knit top pushed invitingly down past her shoulders; and more, many more. K'ing passed through their ranks in growing amazement at the variety of seduction which presented itself in this short strip of land.

Then there were the hawkers. Every city, K'ing had by now learned, had its *casbah,* its patch of interdicted streets where, in return for foreswearing the protection of the public authorities, the traveller could pick up anything he wanted—at a price. In Los Angeles that patch centered, apparently, on the Sunset Strip. To his left a young man with glazed eyes and a long fringed jacket was shaking a handful of glass vials and muttering, as if they comprised an incantation, the names of his wares: "Grass, hash, speeders, ludes, crystal..." Across the pavement from him a wizened old lady with an ancient New York Yankees baseball cap was passing out religious leaflets that promised the Kingdom of God was at hand. A little further down the block a strangely well-scrubbed young couple attempted to interest passers-by in the leather and metal goods they were constructing on the spot. Every so often a policeman would urge these unlicensed peddlers to move on, and they would move a few feet down the walk and set up the impromptu shop again.

Silver and amber, porphyry and gold, all were for sale on the Strip. As readily available as lust and murder, joy and the illusion of joy.

From every open door music blared. The Beatles vied with the Kinks and the Shirelles. Bizarre Balinese scales ran into the conventions of the classical symphony. Ouds and tablas appeared like exotic plants at doorway after doorway. From the street K'ing heard the sound of small bells.

Lights in every color of every rainbow ever imagined by Man assailed his senses. Smells mixed like a vast sensual ragout Incense and pitch and French Fry grease, vermillion and cerise, the clatter of wooden blocks and the tinkle of chains...

He was vaguely conscious of the presence of naked bodies. He tried to focus on something within the crush of humanity, and became aware that almost every other establishment along the walk was a topless dance club. Through smoky glass he could dimly make out the shapes of unclothed female forms. In front husky young men in bright shirts and tight pants announced the attractions within:

"Step right in, men. Step right in. There's plenty of lovely girls to go around. You'll see it all, boys—no holds barred in here! Just two dollars. Sit at the bar and look straight up into the loveliest bit of snatch this side of Hawaii. The amazing Miss Tina. Come right in. They're letting it all hang out. Come and feast your eyes..."

An orange shirt his own height stepped in front of him, blocking the path. "How about you, sir? Want to see some great pussy?"

K'ing waved the hawker away and walked on.

The crowd moved about him like a great turgid stream, moiling, spurting and then relaxing, going somewhere, nowhere, who knew where or why.

The faces were blank or agitated, the bodies were stiff or else they jounced along with exaggerated ease, like street-boppers showing off their strides even when alone. The motion was more like white water than a flow. K'ing thought of the river of his dream, awash with a broken treasure hoard of silver and gold.

Sleepwalkers and preeners. K'ing felt lost in this jittery, aimless crowd, lost and almost hostile. That bothered him. This was Kak's country, to be sure. Best to find what he needed fast and get out...

Then he saw it.

Across the street. A large red sign, swung from a post that protruded over the sidewalk and creaked in the light evening wind.

Abraxas.

Without thinking he stepped between two parked cars into the street. He began to stride quickly toward the sign, and then hesitated, some vestigial element of urban savvy admonishing him at the last second against the traffic. He stopped.

But the cars stopped too. A few feet from him a line of automobiles, which only a second before had been screeching around a gradual bend just ahead of him, had halted to let him pass. He shrugged and crossed the street in the middle of the block, amazed that in the midst of this chaos some conventions were still, as if by rote, observed.

The sign swung on unoiled hinges, sending an eerie raspy whine into the night. K'ing pushed open the bare black door and walked in.

It was dark and quiet in the shop. A heavy cloud of frankincense smoke filled the small room, and the strains of a Gregorian chant, sung horribly off key, came from a speaker in the ceiling. The proprietor had not yet appeared, so K'ing took a moment to inspect his surroundings.

One wall of the room was a library. K'ing was surprised to see a copy of the *Tao Te Ching* under a sign which read "The Orient" but aside from that he recognized none of the texts. Black Magic had always been Kak's forte, not his, and he was not upset at his ignorance.

The opposing wall was filled with dozens of large apothecary jars, in each of which lay a different colored powder. Incenses, K'ing supposed. For what bizarre rites Zedak only knew.

Before the far wall was a glass-enclosed counter. Whereas the other walls, as well as the floor and the ceiling, were covered in black fabric, this one was finished in a shiny metallic surface—perhaps smoked glass, perhaps silver, he was not sure. A large cross, inverted, hung on either side of a central doorway, before which hung a deep crimson curtain. In front of the doorway was the counter. In it K'ing could see the usual accoutrements of Black Magic: candlesticks, bowls, knives, ritual swords, medallions. All in silver. On top of it two huge candles burned; acrid frankincense smoked in a dish.

His eyes scanned the case quickly for a mate to the small object he now clutched in his pocket. But there was nothing resembling it.

Suddenly the curtain behind the case parted, and into the room walked the most nervous person K'ing had ever seen. He was tall but rather stocky, and he leaned forward when he spoke as if he were afraid his listener might depart unexpectedly, so that his posture reminded one of a penguin's. His sallow face showed signs of adolescent acne. He had tried to cover up the blemishes by growing a beard, and then undone half his work by trimming it so thin that K'ing had the impression someone had merely rubbed Mascara along his jawline. His eyes were a kind of muddy grey, and they looked everywhere but at K'ing as he approached. He leaned on the glass counter and the young Master saw that the man had tried to give an impression of physical solidity by wearing leather gauntlets at his wrists. The attempt had not been successful. K'ing walked up to the case and tried to catch his eye.

The man smiled weakly and asked in an unctuous voice tinged with the fear that K'ing had seen outside: "May I help you, sir?"

"I hope so," K'ing replied. He reached into his pocket and withdrew the object he had snatched from the retreating assassin

86

the night before. It caught the light of the large ceremonial candles as he laid it on the glass. "Have you ever seen one of these before?"

The man's tremulous expression and the strain that showed in his thin lips as he tried to keep them from quivering told K'ing all he wanted to know. When the man started to utter a denial, K'ing cut him off short.

"All right, obviously you have. Now, perhaps you can help me, as you say. I wish to find the owner of this piece. He is... let us say an acquaintance... and I wish to return it to him."

"But I have told you, sir, I have never seen one of these before."

Normally King's habitual generosity of mind, his impeccable sense of fairness and politeness, would have prevented him from pressing the frightened man further against his consent. He had no desire to bully him if he could obtain the information he needed in another manner.

But this was a special case. In three days it would be the Equinox, and what dire forces Kak would then be ready to unleash on the unsuspecting populace of Los Angeles, perhaps even the twelve of Zhamballah did not know. K'ing knew that he could not afford to waste more time with this sad example of humanity. Sometimes, Lin Fong had said, the fox can learn from the lion.

Deliberately the young Master picked up the talon from the case. He held it in his hand gingerly, as if weighing it, and then turned it so that the sharp points faced the nervous proprietor. The man's face whitened.

"Now listen to me. I do not wish to harm you if I can avoid it. But if you refuse to help me I will do so. You should be able to see that I am not blind. I am not so blind that I cannot recognize fear when it is a yard away from me across a counter. I see it now. I see it in your face. And I see also that what has frightened you is not my humble presence, but the apparition of this strange little object." He shook it back and forth in front of the gaping mouth.

"Perhaps you are afraid that if I extract information from you regarding this... this ornament... you will be in danger. Is that what you are afraid of, my friend? That someone will take revenge on you for aiding me?"

The man nodded mutely.

"Well, I will do the best I can for you. I will tell you what I will do. If you tell me where I can find the owner of the talon, I promise to breathe a word of it to no one. I promise you that not even the worst tortures of Satan's most artful disciples"—he cast a sneering glance around the tiny room—"will force me to divulge your name. All right?"

The man hesitated. "And if I don't tell you?"

K'ing breathed deeply, grimaced slightly as the acrid scent of the burning powder began to annoy him. "In that case," he said, "I will use this talon to pick out each of your eyes in turn. I will deposit them in one of these beautiful silver chalices and I will watch you eat them."

It was a cheap shot, K'ing knew, and he had some trouble keeping the corners of his mouth from wrinkling. He watched the man's pale face develop a tic as he spoke. Yes, it was just the kind of theatricality that weaklings like this responded to. Besides, he had no time for finesse.

And it worked. The man's head began to bob up and down as if of its own accord, and his muddy eyes grew wide. "All right," he said. "All right."

"Thank you," K'ing said.

"There used to be a cult around here a long time ago called the Cult of the Vulture..."

"I know about that," K'ing interrupted. "And I have no time to listen to it again. Who and where?"

"A crazy old Indian. Name is Blueheels. Jay Blue-heels, I think; yes, that's right, Jay. Jay Blueheels. Lives out near Death Valley, I think."

"You think?"

"Yes, yes, that's right. Death Valley. Place called Jimson Flats. He knows about this, he'll be able to help you. But listen, don't ever tell him who sent you, remember, you promised? Don't tell nobody."

"My lips are sealed," said K'ing as he opened the door behind him.

The young Master walked a block down the Strip to a phone booth, where the yellow pages directed him to a nearby car rental agency. For the first time since he had arrived in California, he was sorry he had left the Ferrari in New York.

K'ing did not see the door to Abraxas open once again immediately after he had left. He did not see a slim, short man with a long purple cloak enter the shop. He did not see the penguin's face pale again in horror and consternation as he stared into the snub barrel of the new visitor's .38. He did not hear the short spurt that sent a bullet through the penguin's forehead, or the clatter of silver as the falling body knocked over a candlestick, or the hiss of the incense which trickled down on him like propitiatory sand.

CHAPTER SEVEN. *THE ROAD TO*
JIMSON FLATS

K'ing had been on the road for an hour. It was now almost two A.M., and he was not sure how long the truck had been following him. In the confusion of light and metal that was the Los Angeles freeway system he had noticed nothing peculiar about the widely spaced pair of headlamps that began to appear at irregular intervals in his rear-view mirror as soon as he hit the Hollywood Freeway. They were one pair out of a thousand, and the young Master, his mind intent on reaching a small town two hundred miles North by daylight, had paid them no special attention.

But now that he was out of the sprawling kaleidoscope of the metropolitan area, he could ignore them no longer. At a steady distance of about a hundred yards they kept doggedly on his tail, and at this point K'ing was not inclined to mark their presence up to coincidence. Any of Kak's people might have seen him go into the little occult shop; any of them might be sent against him now. He glanced in the mirror. The lights kept their distance.

He decided to test his suspicions. Gradually he increased the pressure on the accelerator, and slowly but steadily the big car heaved faster into the night. The surge of power gave him a feeling of indefinable pleasure: not, to be sure, the sense of exhilaration in the mere presence of Power that driving a machine like this one would have given his arch enemy, but a certain contented animation all the same. He was glad he had fought down his distaste for the oppressive materialism of the Californian subculture and specified a brand he knew would give him the speed he so desperately needed tonight. A car, too, that would give him the physical shield he might be grateful for in case something on the desert road ahead— or behind, he thought grimly—was unfriendly to Blue Circle Masters. The Cadillac hummed beneath him, and its huge tires whined on the asphalt as the speedometer needle rose.

K'ing's sharp vision picked out a prairie dog a hundred yards ahead, skittering back to his hole as the car's piercing high beams frightened him off the road. On either side of him clumps of rock and cacti whizzed past, grey in the cloudy night.

The needle pointed to eighty. Then ninety, and ninety-five. K'ing held the wheel easily, calmly appreciative of the graceful feel of the machine.

The needle inched toward one hundred. When it reached it, K'ing's foot relaxed and the big car cruised noiselessly. With his hands loose about the leather covering of the wheel, K'ing turned his eyes up briefly toward the mirror.

The lights were still there. They did not seem to have been discouraged by the Cadillac's sudden spurt of energy. K'ing reckoned he had gained ten, maybe fifteen yards on the truck, no more. Well, he thought, that answers my question. Satisfied, he slowly lifted his foot off the pedal and the needle dropped smoothly back to eighty. The truck kept its distance.

They were, K'ing figured, about thirty miles North of Barstow. The land had been dipping gradually for some time, and the wind that whipped in through the open vent window was beginning to taste like the harsh dryness of the desert. K'ing hit a button at his left elbow and the vent swung closed. He hit another button over his right knee and the whirr of a small motor told him that the car rental man had not lied when he said that Avis always kept their cars, including the air conditioners, in good working order.

About a hundred and fifty miles to go. Two, two and a half hours at the most.

It was plenty of time to get there before dawn. K'ing figured he had an hour or so of grace. He might as well use it trying to get whatever he could out of the Red Circle agent behind him. If the guy had come from Kak, then he would know where Kak was, and K'ing reminded himself grimly that, with only two days before the Equinox, he really had no more of a lead on his arch enemy's whereabouts than the name of a "crazy old Indian" who lived at a waterstop somewhere in the middle of the desert. And what if Jay Blueheels *didn't* know how to get to the Vulture people? K'ing would have made a nightlong journey for nothing, and wasted another precious day.

He decided his best bet would be to confront the trucker Kak had set on his tail. There was no telling how long he planned to maintain that comfortable hundred-yard distance, and as long as he was that far away he was of no use to the Blue Circle Master. No, K'ing would have to find a way to make him play his hand now.

If he had a hand to play, that was. It might simply be Kak's intention to keep the tail on him to unnerve him. That had been the pattern of his enemy's contacts with him so far here in California.

The attack by the three thugs and the (perhaps unplanned) attack by the man in the purple cloak both suggested the same thing: that Kak was not willing or ready to face him directly yet—that he was buying time, and at the same time needling him, by sending these sporadic annoyances against him.

Perhaps, then, the trucker had no move to make. Perhaps he intended to keep his distance all night, just to keep K'ing's mind occupied. Perhaps he was not even a Red Circle agent at all, but just a hired thug like the assassins who had struck at Patty Keele's apartment.

The desert started to swallow him up. A hundred yards behind him the pair of lights glared steadily.

If speed could not bring the trailer on, maybe slowing down would do it. K'ing lightened his touch on the accelerator and let the big car roll gradually down.

Sixty, fifty, forty, thirty-five.

At twenty-five K'ing looked again in the rear-view mirror. The truck had kept its distance as perfectly as if it were tied to the Cadillac by an invisible length of inflexible cord. A hundred yards away it matched K'ing's speed precisely.

The young Master lifted his right foot off the long pedal and brought it down hard on the one in the center. The car shuddered to a stop as the power brakes caught. Over the quiet whirring of the air conditioner K'ing could hear, whining through the desert silence, the asthmatic clutching of the big rig's air brakes, the squeal of its tires. He did not have to look in the mirror to confirm that the truck had come to a halt a hundred yards behind.

He waited. The possibilities were few. He could resume the journey, in which case he was sure that the trailer would merely take up where he had left off. He could wait here and see if his immobility could draw the man out. But that would waste valuable time. He could jam the transmission in reverse and take the guy on face to face. A feasible choice, that one, but K'ing had no desire to engage in false heroics while he was in an automobile, however sturdy, and his potential antagonist was in a rig five times its size. From the way the man had been shifting up and down in perfect synchronization with K'ing's own erratic stops and starts, the young Master knew that the trucker knew his machine well. He did not want to take him on on the road if there was another way. And getting out of the car would be no good either. The driver could just gun the big rig off into the desert and K'ing would be left standing. And looking pretty stupid.

No, there had to be a better way. Finesse, that was what he wanted. He hit the air conditioner button again and the small motor stopped. Now only the hum of the idling engine broke the silence of the desert dark. His lights caught the eyes of a coyote fifty yards up the road, and the animal bounded into the dark with a yelp. K'ing's eyes followed it a few feet off the road, and then—as if the animal had itself presented him with the answer—he smiled broadly, nodded a mute acknowledgment. "Of course," he whispered. The whole trouble here, he thought, was that the man who should be following was being followed, and-the one who should be doing the leading was being led. With a short chuckle K'ing punched the drive button and the long hood jumped before him into the night. A quick glance in the mirror told him that the trucker had started up again too.

The Cadillac was cruising at eighty again in thirty seconds. K'ing checked the mirror one more time to assure himself that the truck had reestablished its distance. Then he jerked the leather-jacketed wheel sharply to the right and the car swerved off the road toward the East in a shower of sand. The big wheels cut into the dry-caked earth as K'ing pressed hard on the accelerator.

Ten yards out he cut the lights. Cacti and rocks whipped past and he dodged them masterfully, his powerful hands loose and flexible on the wheel. The big car responded with precise, quick movements to the boy's deft touch.

A hundred yards. A hundred and fifty. Two hundred. The sand whipped up behind him in little cat's whiskers as the Cadillac swayed like a belly dancer among the cacti. Half a mile away K'ing could see a bank of huge craggy outcroppings looming grey in the dim light of a half-clouded moon. Behind him... nothing.

Nothing. The ruse had worked, apparently. The trucker's orders, or his imagination, did not extend this far. K'ing smiled and slowed the car. A few hundred yards from the first of the large outcroppings, he stopped and looked back.

The truck had not left the road. It was stopped a mile away due West. Its beams still illuminated the asphalt of the road North.

But then a third light came on, and this one began to turn. Slowly, methodically, it moved right and began to scan the dark off the road. Without wasting time to think K'ing gunned the powerful motor again and the car shot out toward the outcropping. With a jerk first to the right and then to the left, the young Master found himself on the far side of the peak, just as the beam of the trucker's searchlight reached the face nearest the road.

The light lingered a moment on the red rock, then moved on. Behind the rock K'ing smiled again. The first part of his plan had gone all right.

When the scanning light moved back toward the road, K'ing gunned the motor a third time, wheeled the car toward the South, and shot off again into the desert. The reflexes that had so many times saved him from assassins now served him well as he weaved the Cadillac artfully through the dark of the desert, dodging the sparse brush, coming within inches of jagged rocks, scattering the nocturnal inhabitants of the wasteland before him.

In five minutes, he calculated, he was five miles to the South. He did not think that the trucker would leave immediately. Give him five minutes more at least. Then he would give up the search and be off. Off, K'ing hoped, to Kak Nan Tang.

Only this time K'ing would be behind him. His headlights cut, his distance great enough so that the man would not hear even the low whine of the big tires, K'ing would be the follower.

He swerved the big car to the right and in another two minutes was back on the road. He turned right again, completing the circle, and proceeded cautiously up the dark highway.

As soon as he hit the road he checked the odometer. When he had put another four and a half miles on it, he slowed the car to a crawl.

Yes. There it was. K'ing's eyes picked up the rig's lights, fixed ahead now, from nearly a mile away. He inched forward a couple of hundred yards, then cut the motor to an idle, and waited to see what the trucker would do.

As he had expected, he did not have to wait long. He checked his watch. It was two-thirty. The entire ruse had taken less than a half hour, and now he had the tail where he wanted him.

The rig moved out, its lights plowing through the night a half mile ahead of the lightless Cadillac. K'ing settled back, almost enjoying the ride. It was easier here, on the road. Even without lights the big car took the gradual bends easily, as K'ing's mind translated the curves a half-mile ahead into what was coming up right in front of him. In a few minutes he had got this knack of driving ahead down pat, and he relaxed in body if not in mind as the truck led him through the night.

Even in the middle of the night K'ing could feel that they were getting deep into hot and arid terrain. The air was thick, dusty, and even at this hour the heat was stifling. He was glad for the air-conditioning, for Death Valley was no fit place for human habitation. He wondered what this Jay Blue-heels, who lived in the desert, was like—and what he would have to say to him. He wondered, now that the trucker was leading him straight to Kak—or so he hoped—whether he would have to talk to the old Indian at all.

After about an hour the truck abruptly stopped. K'ing braked the Cadillac to a halt, cut the engine, and narrowed his eyes to make out what was going on a half-mile ahead.

The trucker was getting out of the cab, climbing down, walking over to something on the side of the road.

A pipe of some sort. A pump, maybe.

Of course. K'ing nodded his head in mild self-deprecation. It surprised him that, although his knowledge of the Tao and its strange ways in the world of men was probably as acute and extensive as that of any one he knew alive, he sometimes missed the little things. The trucker was merely filling his radiator from one of the many water spigots that the National Park Service had seen fit to install in this bleakest and least hospitable of all the National Monuments. K'ing leaned back, closed his eyes for the briefest second of concentration on the eternal wisdom of Zhamballah, and opened them again. He waited.

Then, suddenly, he realized his mistake. Silently he cursed himself, hoped it was not too late. This would be the perfect time! The man was out of the protection of the cab, he would have to replace the can at the spigot, it might take a minute or two... this was the time to strike! Impatiently he flicked the motor on again and prepared to floor the accelerator.

And then he hesitated. Perhaps, he thought, it would be wiser simply to wait, to follow the truck as he had been doing for an hour, to wait until it brought him to Kak.

But how did he know for certain that the truck was on its way to Kak?

Of course he knew. Where else would the man be going?

But if he were not, then K'ing would be wasting valuable time. It was best to confront the man directly if he could. He would do it now! The man would tell him, would take him there himself!

He wondered if this way were the surer one. Play the waiting game, or strike? The man might not be as easy to persuade as the pudgy character in the occult shop, and then K'ing would have forfeited his chance to follow him unseen to Kak's headquarters. Then he would have to rely on Jay Blueheels alone.

But then he would be no worse off than he was right now...

His foot made the decision before his mind had time to carry out the reasoning. The Cadillac shot into the night. K'ing's left hand hit the lights and they came up, washing the road ahead like a flare. Maybe, he thought, that would startle the man enough so that he would take the extra few seconds K'ing needed....

K'ing's lights whirled the man around, and K'ing saw him spurt to the cab.

It was too late. K'ing's few moments of hesitation had given the man all the time he needed to cap the radiator, hurl the can from him, and remount the cab. As the Cadillac screeched to a stop beside the truck and the lithe form of the young Master leaped out, the big rig was already lurching forward in a mad rumble of gears.

K'ing leaped desperately at the retreating truck, but his grasping fingers could find no hold. They scraped down the siding of the trailer with the eerie screech of metal on glass. The truck's wheels sang mockingly as he tumbled to the ground.

He was up again before the truck had gone ten yards. Up and into the waiting Cadillac, and his foot hit the accelerator as if he were crushing a scorpion underfoot. His body shook with the rage that his mind would not permit him to feel.

There was no time for finesse now. Now it would have to be done the direct way. The hard way. K'ing had lost this round. Now he would have to go for the throat. If he allowed the Red Circle agent to get completely away, he would be left only with the Indian, and he had no way of knowing how informative he might be.

The Cadillac closed the gap between K'ing and the trucker in less than a minute. The heavy automatic transmission had an important advantage in the short run over the grinding, multi-geared trailer, and now K'ing was grateful for it. He came up fast behind the big rig, floored the pedal into passing gear, and whipped the car out into the left lane. In a second he was chest to chest with the trucker.

K'ing was not thinking now. His body was issuing orders on instinct, and his mind obeyed with the blind trust that only perfect allies can have for each other. He did not know what he was going to do when he overtook the truck, but only that action—a show of force, an attack, however dangerous it was for him—was needed, and his body tightened itself beautifully for the job at hand.

The speedometer read ninety-four as he came up abreast to the cab. The trucker was going to make it into a race. All right, K'ing was ready for that. He bore down on the pedal, his hands easy on the wheel, one eye on the bending road, one on the massive vehicle to his right.

Tires squealed loud as the two vehicles went into a long bend. K'ing was on the inside, and he knew that would put him at a serious disadvantage if this aimless race suddenly turned into a battering contest. The bigger vehicle would have the greater leverage, and by simply drifting slightly to its left it could force the Cadillac off the road. At over ninety miles an hour, that wasn't what K'ing had in mind.

But it was exactly what the trucker had in mind. One second the two were speeding madly along the gradually tightening bend. The next second, without warning, the cab twitched six inches toward the car, and K'ing heard the scrape of metal on metal, felt the steady, impassive nudge that told him the man was trying to drive him into the desert.

Good, he thought, at least now we know where we stand. The two-hour cat-and-mouse game was over; now the real fight would begin. K'ing's spirit soared within him as his strained muscles got him ready for the belated confrontation.

The instant the wheels of the huge rig touched the car's frame K'ing cut his power and braked. The rig hurtled in front of him, missing the front fender of the Cadillac by inches, and just barely keeping on me road as the curve tightened ahead. Round two, thought the young Master. That's one and one.

The road straightened out. K'ing hit the gas again, came up alongside the bobbing rig. This time, when the big cab inched toward him, K'ing floored the accelerator, and the Cadillac shot ahead, grazing the fender of the truck. In a moment he was at the side of the cab again, dodging, playing, weaving.

This was the kind of game that K'ing excelled at.

Even in this unfamiliar territory, handling a car twice the size of his own Ferrari, the young Master showed the steady nerves, the balanced sense of calm exhilaration, that had so impressed Joe Corcoran in his battle with the three thugs.

It was true, as Lin Fong had said: if a man's body is his own, then he can make anything else his own as well. If it is not, then nothing else can aid him.

K'ing used the car now as part of his body. When he swayed to the right, it was with the easy grace of a gliding bird; when he shot ahead it was with the force and conviction of a charging ram; when he dropped back it was with the assurance of the man who knew just where his feet were planted. The trucker weaved and spurted erratically, and K'ing knew that his dodging motions were having the desired effect. The cab lurched crazily from side to side. Perhaps, thought K'ing, a few more minutes of this and the man would stop. Then we can talk like sensible human beings...

They had been moving so fast that K'ing had not had time to take a good look at his antagonist. Now, as the road stretched clear for more than a mile ahead, he jerked his head quickly to the right and tried to find in the driver's face the explanation for a host of unanswered questions. With his hands steadying the wheel, his calm blue eyes assayed the features of the man who had, he was sure, been sent to keep him from his destined appointment with the leader of the Red Circle.

What he saw brought him up sharp.

For a second he doubted the evidence of his own eyes. He stole another glance. He blinked.

Yes. It was him. He was not mistaken.

The white hair might have belonged to any number of men. Even any number of hired assassins. But that pale, gaunt face, and those gruesome pink eyes could belong to only one man on this earth.

The White One.

K'ing's breath caught in his throat as he realized the meaning of his discovery. If The White One was here, Kak's plans would be big indeed. It was now all the more important for him to take this murderer alive, to get out of him by any means necessary the whereabouts of the Red Circle encampment.

99

But could any power on earth take The White One alive? K'ing recalled grimly that even The Moor, who was certainly his equal as a fighter, had only been able to fight the albino assassin to a standstill. He seemed to exist in some untouchable realm beyond the strictures of lesser men—beyond the will, even, of the Red Circle.

No. K'ing would not think that. The White One was a man, just like him. Powerful, devious, dangerous. But a man.

And a man may be killed.

Or saved from killing. A man could be captured. K'ing bent all his massive energies to the task at hand, as the two speeding shapes hurtled through the night.

One more glance to the right revealed his enemy's cruel face again. K'ing needed a second to consider. Deliberately, as the hulk of metal bore down on him again, he dropped back. Mindlessly he hit the high beams as he did so, and they shot full on the outside rear-view mirror that hung from the window of the cab.

In that instant the white face of the killer was framed in the tiny circle of glass. For a second K'ing had the impression that the truck's mirror was suspended not from the side of the cab, but in space, beyond space, beyond all time and all space and all thought of earthly dimension. Weightless and untouchable it hung somewhere between heaven and hell, and from its glistening center, from within a piercing field of light, the awful visage of the driver grinned like a mocking skull. K'ing thought he could hear, far off, the laughter of a million voices, the harsh, rasping trill of the dead, calling, beckoning, welcoming him as their own.

He shook his head angrily and the vision passed. Again he set his mind to the business at hand. The speedometer hovered just under a hundred. The huge machine just in front of him darted from side to side. He gripped the wheel and his face was dark with conviction.

Then he saw it. Half a mile ahead the road turned into a bridge, the first of many over the shallow canyons that laced the desert floor in silent testimony to where the rivers once had been. It was not a deep chasm, or long, that the bridge had to cross. But it was enough of a disruption of the regularity of the hard-packed floor that it had convinced the Park Service to span it.

Even from this distance it was obvious to K'ing that only one vehicle could pass over it at once. The thin trickle of traffic that passed through this desolated spot evidently did not justify building a two-lane bridge, and K'ing saw that either he or the truck would be forced off the road at a hundred miles an hour if they attempted to cross it together.

The White One had seen the bridge too, and immediately the battering contest became a race again.

Ten seconds. Twelve. Thirteen. Fourteen. Fifteen. K'ing counted rapidly as the big car held the ground and the truck tried to keep on a steady line beside it.

Twenty yards from the narrow structure K'ing saw that the truck's slight edge on him would send it clattering onto the boards of the bridge a split-second before him.

He had no time to think. His body acted. Somewhere deep within his consciousness he knew that it would be fatal to run the race out to the end. The corner of his eye told him that the two or three inches that the truck had on him were, at this speed, all The White One needed. He forgot about the bridge and inched imperceptibly to the left.

The truck's heavy wheels struck the boards like thunder as K'ing urged a last drop of power out of his straining automobile. The Cadillac's wheels bit the sand at the edge of the ravine and K'ing sailed into the air with the awful lumbering grace of a demolition derby stuntman. He gripped the wheel tightly and braced himself for the landing. It seemed a lifetime he was suspended in the air just to the left of the span. Then...

THUNK!

The heavy car landed in a small explosion of sand. Bolts creaked underneath. K'ing pressed still harder on the accelerator, and hurtled North again through the night. The speedometer read a hundred and three. Beside him the already ashen face of the hired killer seemed to turn whiter yet as he realized that K'ing was still in the game.

But there was another ravine up ahead, and this one, K'ing could see, the Cadillac could not jump. In one of those inexplicable natural accidents, the old gods who had laid out the valley floor had plowed a trench hundreds of yards wide and well over fifty deep in the middle of this flat plain. It was looming up quickly now, and K'ing saw he would have either to sweat another five miles per hour out of his already tortured engine, or let The White One take this one for himself... and he did not think the car was up to another inch an hour. K'ing could hear a tell-tale wheezing from under the hood, the first hint of the mechanical cough that said the engine had already overextended itself.

The metal guardrail of the long bridge gleamed dully in the moonlight, like a pair of silver sickles. It was coming up fast now, and in another second K'ing would have to drop back.

Unless...

Yes! K'ing could see the bridge clearly now. This one was a double-laned one! With renewed vigor he pushed his foot against the pedal. Neck and neck he came up again to the cab...

The Cadillac and the truck hit the metal surface with a clatter like a building breaking.

The wheel did not move. K'ing's nerves held. The car sped forward smoothly.

But then, from the right, K'ing sensed a new threat. He had no need to look to confirm his suspicions. The slight tap of metal against metal told him that here, fifty yards above a dessicated stream, The White One was going to make another bid for glory. He was going to try to drive K'ing right through the thin railing, onto the stones below.

At a hundred miles an hour each tiny motion is magnified a thousand times, and the least mistake in calculation can be the difference between life and death. K'ing knew that, and so did the killer in the cab. That is why his attempt to unseat the young Master seemed tentative, edgy, almost too calm to believe. Gradually he inched the heavy vehicle closer to the speeding Cadillac, until less than a foot remained between the side of the car and the railing which separated them both from death.

Had K'ing's nerves been those of a normal human being, he would now have been dead. His body would be lying at the bottom of a dry chasm somewhere in tie middle of Death Valley, food for vultures and snakes. Had he flinched the least bit in that fearful minute on the bridge, the world would have lost its greatest living Master of Kung Fu.

But K'ing did not flinch. The boy who had already looked on death a thousand times, and had laughed in its face, kept his hands steady on the wheel and his eyes on the road. When he felt the first tentative nudge, he dropped back so slightly that even The White One's keen sense could not pick up the motion. With calm, heartless deliberation he drew his attacker out, set him up for the kill as a Judo expert might set up an opponent.

"Use your enemy's own strength against him." Lin Fong's words had never seemed so appropriate, or so wise, as at this moment.

The assassin's strength at this moment was his need to have K'ing dead. The Urge to Kill. K'ing knew this, and it was because he himself lacked that urge to such a marked degree that he found himself still alive at this moment. Now he used that urge against the would-be killer.

A slight pressure on the accelerator, and the Cadillac moved forward. A slight turn of the wrist, and it moved right. The two were half way across the narrow, swaying bridge when the handsbreadth between them closed, and the racing wheels touched in a flurry of sparks.

But so expert were the two drivers, so nerveless and so intent upon their individual quests, that the shock threw neither off balance. The tension held.

The wheels did not lock. Side to side they whined across the chasm, swaying imperceptibly. The pressure between them was just enough to prevent either vehicle from gaining another inch, as long as the driving wheels were kept locked straight ahead.

But now K'ing pulled his trump card. So gradually that even his acute sense had trouble identifying the shift in energy, he upset the delicate balance. At close to a hundred miles per hour even the slightest lateral movement was an invitation to disaster, but the young Master's nerves never betrayed hesitancy as he increased the pressure against the rig. The White One, he knew, would have to compensate or be driven through the right hand railing. When he did K'ing would make his move.

The response was not long in coming. K'ing felt the heavy machine to his right stiffen with the increase of pressure, as though the metal itself were in revolt against the intrusion on its already limited space.

Then, as gradually as K'ing had done, the killer urged his wheels left.

Within the few seconds it took the speeding machines to cover another two hundred yards the pressure had increased to a mind-shattering extent. Sparks flew like luminous hail. The screech

103

of the tires was deafening. The two vehicles were locked in a super-sensitive, deadly embrace.

With less than a quarter mile to go K'ing made his move. He waited until he felt the power of the other vehicle to be at its peak. In another fraction of a second, he knew, his lighter car would be able to withstand the tension no longer. In that fraction he could be hurtling over the side. He braced himself, locked his powerful arms about the wheel...

Now!

K'ing's right foot stamped with unnerving ease on the power brake. The big car bucked violently, and the steering wheel was a thing alive. It took all of K'ing's strength to hold it still. In seconds the Cadillac's speed plummeted violently. At eighty K'ing knew he had the big machine under control.

But The White One had lost it. When the resistance to which the heavy rig had become accustomed suddenly disappeared, the huge wheels twisted sharply and went skidding into the guard rail to the left. The long back end of the trailer began to fishtail and the cab scored the other railing in a long, searing swipe.

K'ing slowed even more, and by the time the Cadillac was doing a comfortable seventy-five the rig had crashed through the first of several retaining posts and was halfway off the bridge.

K'ing smiled with grim satisfaction as he watched the huge mass of metal turn three times in the air and then explode in a paroxysm of flame at the bottom of the canyon. He came off the far end of the bridge at seventy, pulled the car over to the left in another screech of tires, and got out. He walked the few yards back to the edge of the canyon and looked down. The rig was a mass of flame, and the sides of the little canyon shimmered fiercely in the unnatural light. It was obvious that trudging down the steep sides to see if his assailant had survived the crash would be a waste of time. He walked back to the car.

"Well," he thought as the powerful motor pulled him back on the road, "I guess now it'll have to be the Indian."

CHAPTER EIGHT. *JAY BLUEHEELS*

The man at the gas station twenty miles back—"Last Chance Before Perdition" the sign had read—had said it was a ghost town, but Jimson Flats looked like it had never been a town at all, ghosts or no ghosts. Looking at the three tiny ramshackle dwellings—two weathered clapboard houses and an adobe hut—K'ing understood why the man had looked incredulous when he had asked directions to the place.

"The Flats?" he had asked. "Now why the devil would you be wanting to go to the Flats? There ain't nobody there excepting a crazy old Injun name of Blueheels, and if you can get any straight talk out of that one, you're a better man than I am, son. What business you got in Jimson Flats?"

K'ing had been patient with the man's confusion. He had spoken simply. "I wish to speak to this man Blueheels. You say he still lives there?"

"He lives there all right. Comes in here once every few weeks for supplies, then he's out in the sun again, sooner than you can say howdy. Been out in that damn sun too long, too, if you ask me. Must be why he talks funny like, you know what I mean? You sure it's him you want to see?"

Yes, K'ing had been sure. Now, as he mounted the rickety steps of the first wooden house, he could still see the man's features contort into a worried frown, his hand to his head, as he considered the possibility that he would soon have to be dealing each month with two sun-crazed hermits rather than one.

The first step crumbled beneath him, and K'ing withdrew his foot just in time to escape the deadly jaws of a Gila monster whose retreat from the blazing early morning sun K'ing's intrusion had disturbed. He hopped gingerly over the remaining steps, walked across the narrow porch, and pushed open the door.

The single small room was empty but for a pair of rattlesnakes who had, like their reptilian cousin under the porch, come in to escape the heat. As K'ing entered they slithered rapidly under a broken floorboard and out of sight.

Dust lay thick on the grey, cracked floor and cobwebs hung in soft dirty canopies from each corner. There was not a piece of furniture in the room. The single window which opened East now admitted, through four splintered panes of glass, the first heavy heat of the day. K'ing turned and walked out.

The second wooden dwelling was empty as well. K'ing was surprised to see three heavy iron bars on its lone window, but aside from that it was indistinguishable from the first building. He pushed open the door and walked back into the sunshine.

Across the street—or rather the wagon path that led West from the highway for half a mile until it ended in this crumbling cluster of wood and stone—the adobe gleamed in the sun. K'ing realized now that he should have thought of this first. Anyone who could survive in this heat, no matter how crazy others may think he was, would be wise enough to find shelter within a light-colored structure—something that would reflect the glare of the sun rather than absorbing it. If Jay Blueheels actually did live in this wilderness, this is where he would be. K'ing walked the few steps to the door and knocked on the weathered wood. When he received no response, he pushed lightly on the door and it swung in.

The single room was marginally more inhabitable than the other two. At one end, along the northern wall, lay a sleeping tick. A heavy woven blanket lay on top of this primitive bedding, its rich blues and reds a striking contrast to the general drabness of the room. At the other end of the small enclosure a shallow pit had been scooped out of the earthen floor, and the remains of a fire within it reminded K'ing that nights on the desert were often as chill as the days were hot. He walked to the pit and felt the coals.

Cold.

The old Indian had not been here recently, at least, and K'ing wondered now how much time he could afford to waste waiting for him. He decided to give the old man a few hours anyway. Perhaps he was out foraging for breakfast, and would return soon. Perhaps he was merely an early riser out for a morning walk.

If he was to be here a while, then, the young Master thought, he might as well use the time to good advantage. He walked to the window and pulled down the rough burlap flap that served as a shade, then seated himself on the ground directly in front of the sleeping pallet. He was tired. His body told him that he could not go too much longer without some rest. And yet he was not sleepy. He had felt this way many times before, and when he did any thought of sleeping was merely distractive. What his body needed now was not repose, but peace. The peace that only his

Kung Fu meditations could afford.

His hands placed lightly on his knees, his entire body relaxed in an instant, his spirit sought the Wind that Blows in the Void.

Within moments the oppressive heat of the desert was forgotten. All was forgotten—the fatal encounter with The White One, the vivid mental pictures of corpses daubed with Chinese characters, the vast fluorescent confusion of Los Angeles, even his quest for Kak, receded into an unknown compartment of his mind as the calm his being craved wound its tender coils about him.

Gradually, as his soul glided with the jets and eddies of a gentle, cooling wind, his mind painted for him a picture of the serene, kindly Master who, years ago in another desert, had brought him up to manhood.

For how long K'ing sat in easy concentration he did not know. Time itself stopped as the image of Lin Fong's smiling countenance floated again and again before him. Now they were-laughing and practicing on the desert. Now they sat quietly content after a day's hard exercise, and the boy listened to the sage tell of the old days, the old ways, the awesome heritage the boy was about to receive. Now they sat in silence opposite one another, the wind brushing the old man's robe, their eyes dead, their minds alive to everything and nothing at once. Now the boy opened his eyes, saw the old man smiling calmly at him, pleased at his growth in discipline...

K'ing opened his eyes slowly. In the dim light of dusk, in the faint suggestion of dawn, he watched the ancient eyes of his Master soften and sparkle and smile.

Yet he was faintly conscious of something different, something new. Lin Fong's face was the same, but there was something about him now that...

The blue eyes began to focus. The young Master, his spirit still caught on an impossible wind, gradually came to himself, came back to his body. Back to this day and this space. Back to— he reminded himself where he was—the vast majesty of Death Valley.

His eyes were open now. But the old man before him was not Lin Fong. He was the same, and yet he was entirely different. The eyes sparkled like Lin Fong's, and yet this old man was not his Master.

His face was beardless and his eyes were black. He sat easily across from the young Master, his legs crossed comfortably, his hands folded in his lap. Sandals covered his feet, and the skin beneath the straps was dark, almost black. He wore thin white muslin pants and a loose jacket of the same material. Around his neck hung a string of turquoise beads—the deepest blue K'ing had ever seen. At his waist the tunic was pulled tight by a stout rope, and from the excess length hung more beads—turquoise again, and silver.

The man's features were clean and uncomplicated. Deep black eyes flanked a nose that K'ing recognized as "Roman". The high cheekbones and the fine, rigid jawline suggested a toughness that the gentle eyes belied. His mouth moved easily, as if, although he spoke only when necessary, speaking did not come as a burden to him. A small scar near one corner of the mouth made it seem as if the old Indian were continually on the verge of a grin.

"I am Jay Blueheels," he said. "And you are one day late."

The mystic has a great capacity for wonder, but none at all for surprise. There was little in the world of men that truly shocked the young Master of the Earthly Center. In his few short years as a Blue Circle Master, he had had countless opportunities to discover that what on the surface appeared to be "accidental" or "coincidental" was in fact only a piece of a vast, as yet undisclosed, design. "Chance" played a small role in his vocabulary.

So he was not surprised at his initial encounter with the man who was known, as far south as Los Angeles, as "that crazy old Indian."

He was not surprised that Jay Blueheels had known, by what ministry K'ing felt it superfluous to ask, that he was on his way to Death Valley. He was not surprised that the old man was completely familiar with the history of the Vulture cult, and even with the importance of the Autumn Equinox in its religious calendar.

Nor had K'ing been surprised to discover that, far from being "crazy", as the popular wisdom about the hermit went, Jay Blueheels was a man eminently in control of his senses.

K'ing allowed himself to wonder whether the old Indian's reputation for madness had been concocted by the man himself to keep the curious away from his bleak haunts, or was the inevitable

108

explanation seized upon by men who could not understand in any other way why a human being would wish to forsake the blessings of their civilization for the ancient austerity of Death Valley. But for whatever reason, the idea that Jay Blueheels was, as Joe Corcoran would have put it, a "crackpot", was clearly nothing more than a crazy idea itself.

Now he sat respectfully before the old man, listening. His voice was thin with age, but it rose gradually as he warmed to his tale.

"This is what you must know, young one, before we leave tomorrow to find the Vulture people.

"Many years ago, this desert was rich with grain. The people that lived here lived in peace, and were well and full from the beasts and plants of the land. They worshipped the great Thunderbird, and in return for the sacrifices which they performed each year in his honor, he sent down rain enough for all to eat and drink their fill.

"But in time the people grew lazy, for the comforts which the land had bestowed on them came without their working for them. Because the buffalo was always thick on the plains and the fish heavy in the waters, the men who should have been hunters sat in their tipis and refused to hunt: hunting was child's work now, they said. And so the children were sent out to hunt.

"For a few seasons this was well. So plentiful was the game that a boy could easily kill what in the other places of this land it took a man to kill. Men of thirty summers sat at home with the women, and ate the food given to them by children half your age.

"But soon a strange thing began to happen. Where the fields had been green before, now the summer sun beat down harder on the grain, and yellow showed among the stalks of corn and wheat, and the fields became drier than even the oldest man could remember them ever having been. The animals, who always had fed from the rich fields, now had too little to eat, and they began to move North and South in search of food. When the animals left, the people were left with little to eat—for in their indolence they had not thought to store anything up—and they gradually began to grow hungry and weak. Fear began to stalk the lodges, for none of the people of the tribe had ever experienced hunger before.

"Then a great council was held, and at the council it was agreed that surely the people had in some way offended the great

Thunderbird. Therefore they set about appeasing him so they could eat again. Huge feasts were held, whole animals were burnt and offered to the god where before the choicest parts alone had served.

"At the end of the feasting, however, the people had even less food than before. And still the sky was dry as sand.

"Then, from somewhere out of the East, a young man who wore strange designs on his clothing and spoke in a tongue no one could understand, came into the village. By the use of sign language he made it understood that he was an emissary from the gods, and that he had the answer to their plight. So desperate were the people by this time that they were ready to accept the instructions of anyone who offered the least hope, and so they listened to the scheme of the strange young man.

"He said that the god they had offended was not the Thunderbird, but one whose worship had been neglected in this land for over a hundred seasons. The god's name was Vulture, and in order to appease him the people must now sacrifice half the boy children and half the girl children of the tribe in his honor. Then the rains would come.

"The people obeyed. In one awful night half the children of the tribe were slaughtered to appease the god they now came to call the Deathbird. The night was loud with the wailing of parents, and in the morning the village was littered with dozens of small corpses.

"But the rains did not come. The people waited six days, and still the sky showed no sign of darkening. They went to the young man, and they asked him what this meant. He said that his god was still displeased with their disregard of his worship, and that he now demanded the slaughter of the rest of the tribe's children.

"The people held another great council, and at this council, while they were debating whether or not to sacrifice all their remaining offspring, their prayers were finally answered.

"But not by the god who called himself the Death-bird. For while the council was still sitting, Thunderbird took pity on his people, and appeared in the sky above them, hovering like a huge thundercloud himself. The Vulture god, he said, had tricked them. The young man on whose authority they had thrown away the lives of half their children was in reality the evil god himself, and such was the depth of his viciousness that he would not have been satisfied until every member of the hungry tribe had been sacrificed in his name. For his name, said Thunderbird, was Death, and the death of living things was the blood of life to him.

"Now the people sent up a great wailing and lamentation, and they vowed to revenge themselves on the trickster. But when they made their way to the place where he had been, he was gone. Only a silver talon rested on the spot, in mockery of the foolish people who had destroyed the flower of their tribe on the word of a wicked stranger.

"The people then returned to Thunderbird and pleaded with him to help them find and kill the wrongdoer.

"'You cannot kill a god,' said Thunderbird. 'You cannot even fight one, for it is for the gods to avenge their own wrongs and fight their own wars. But a battle is coming. A great battle. And for the pain and suffering that you have undergone, you will now be able to take some joy. For you will all be present at this battle, and at the end of the battle the Death-bird will trouble you no more.'

"The great bird pointed then to the East, and the people of the tribe turned their faces in that direction. What they saw made them hide their faces in fear and huddle together like sheep before a storm.

"For the horizon was filled with dust, and the dust was moving toward them with the speed of a raging river. Louder and louder the cloud came on, until the sun was nearly blotted out by the thickness of it.

"And then, from the middle of the cloud, emerged the Vulture.

"The black giant's wings stretched from horizon to horizon. A mile in the air he hovered, and his screech was deafening, horrible to hear. His breast and wings were of ebony, his beak and talons of silver. His eyes narrowed, his head fell back haughtily as he rested in the air, waiting for death.

"Gold and green and blue were the colors of Thunderbird's wings. His breast was all of gold, and his beak and talons also. Majestically the colors blazed in the sunlight as he rose to meet the adversary. The people stared in awe as the two giants prepared to do battle.

"The clash of the giant bodies was like the clattering of a million burnished shields. The people threw hands over their ears and averted the frightened children's eyes as the spectacle began.

"Thunderbird swept upward with the grace of the wind and the Vulture's talons scraped the air an inch from his breast. He wheeled toward the sun and came down above the evil god, the gold at his feet spreading and clutching, reaching and darting for the neck.

"But the Vulture skittered from beneath the attack and brought his silver claws up fast. The people gasped as a small ring of red appeared in the gold of Thunderbird's breast. Then he fell back, flapping wings with his face still toward the sun, and his screeching shook the foundations of the earth. His wings went out wide, and the noonday sun was behind them, and the people could see nothing but gold.

"Then he attacked again. The awful voice still searing the air, he dove with his talons extended, and this time it was the Vulture whose body spurted blood. Where the throat met the shoulder red soaked the black of his wing, and his shriek of pain was more terrible to hear than the screaming of a tortured babe.

"The Vulture brought his deadly talons up fast, seeking Thunderbird's eyes. The great god drew back faster than the people's eyes could see, and his own talons met the adversary's, locked with them in a deadly embrace. The ankles of the giant birds were crimson with blood as they scratched and ripped flesh from each other's bodies. Where Thunderbird's blood fell, there the people became suddenly, strangely, calm: for such was the power of the god's life-giving fluid that it animated the very souls of those for whom it was shed.

"But where the Vulture's blood happened to fall, there the people died. The people watching the battle screamed and huddled in groups as, all around them, their kinsmen fell to the ground dead, stained with the deadly crimson of the Deathbird's wounds. Like a shower of poison his blood rained down, killing with aimless abandon.

"Now the Vulture backed off, tearing Thunderbird's legs savagely as he went. He hovered in the air, black against the sun, for a second and then swooped down again. His talons formed a fearful fence before him as his silver beak darted at the great god's eyes. Blood streamed from the side of Thunderbird's head where the deadly beak struck wide.

"And Thunderbird spoke, his voice mighty with the power of godhood, and brought his own beak down. The sound of cym-

112

bals filled the air as the two gigantic beaks struck together. From within a pink mist the noise arose again and again, loud as a mighty waterfall, ringing as the roar of a forest fire. Both the Vulture and Thunderbird were red with their wounds now. Their faces were masks of scarlet, their bodies cloaked and swimming in blood.

"From noon until dusk the great birds fought, tireless and savage. For half the length of the sun's passage through the sky, the people quivered below. They never saw the sun, all that bloody day. The soaring, darting forms of the gods had entirely blocked it from view. In the middle of the day the fight had brought darkness. The sun passed its journey unseen as the great bodies hid the sky.

"As dusk approached the battle drew to a close. Though the sun was hidden the people sensed the coming of the end, and held their breaths in anticipation of the conclusion that would make them slaves to the deadly will of the Vulture, or free people once again. Grimly they avoided the corpses at their feet, silently they urged Thunderbird on to victory.

"The warring gods separated a last time. Thunderbird was to the South, the Deathbird to the North. They embraced the horizon with their wings. They prepared to strike.

"And then, in those few seconds as the giant forms gathered strength for a last onslaught, the setting sun shone through the space between their bodies.

"With a single cry of awe the people covered their faces as the blinding rays washed about them. Never before had they felt the sun so strongly. In that second of brightness at the close of a black afternoon, their eyes were closed and, for the first time, they saw the magic beauty of the fight in its full glory.

"And the gods attacked. Darkness covered the earth as the birds came together. The sound of enormous wings filled the dry air. The people trembled.

"The Vulture's deadly claws raked Thunderbird's chest, and the gold showed carnadine. Thunderbird swept one foot in a wide, clean arc, and his talon dangled black feathers. The Vulture leaped forward, his beak seeking the eyes of his opponent. Thunderbird averted them an instant before the silver spikes struck. He squealed majestically and leaped through the air. His talons dug in to the burnished silver of his adversary's breast, and held. Frantically the Vulture attempted to shake him off, but Thunderbird held on. The air was loud with the screeching of the gods, the plain was red with their wounds.

"When the Vulture realized that he would not be able to shake off his attacker, he brought his own talons up sharp from underneath, and they locked savagely into the gold of Thunderbird's belly. Throughout the setting of the sun the two gods stayed locked in deadly embrace, their beaks darting back and forth faster than the people's eyes could follow, their wicked claws seeping ever deeper into each other's bodies.

"At sunset the Vulture fell. His entire body was red now, and his strength was gone. Thunderbird felt his body go limp, felt the shudder that meant his victory was close, and he let the giant body go. Lamely the Deathbird flapped broken wings, and his great form rose into the air. Thunderbird hovered nearby, alert, waiting.

"Again the giant birds separated, and again the Western horizon showed between their bodies. Now the sun was a dot of red half-way behind a huge rock formation. With a last horrible screech the defeated god made his way there, and came to rest on the top of the crag. His giant wings folded now as if at rest, his black form became a silhouette against the red of the dying sun. Thunderbird hovered above his people, watching his enemy's retreat.

"Then the Vulture spoke. Horrible and sonorous his voice came over the flat of the desert. Haughtily he raised his wings and let them fall. Then he cursed the people he had lost to Thunderbird.

"'Half your children, people of the valley, you have given me. The other half I will wait for. You have beaten me now, but the Vulture never dies. The Vulture cannot be killed, but only put to rest. I go to rest now. For how long you cannot know. But this curse I say to you, and it will make your dreams dark until I come again.

"'The next harvest in this land will be a harvest of hate. A harvest of death and darkness. Look for no other fruits from this land, for it has borne its last pear tree, its last pomegranate. This valley is now my valley, and I call it henceforth the Valley of Death. From it I banish you and all your children. Exiles you will be now, cursed to wander forever, cursed never to find the land where once you lived in peace and plenty. From this day forward let no plant grow here, from this day forward let peace be forgotten in the land.

"'One more thing I say to you. You will not know how long I may sleep. But when I come again, it will be amid cries and wail-

114

ings greater than any you have heard before. *When the Vulture wakes, the dark harvest will begin!'*

"Then, suddenly, he was gone. The people did not see him go, and whether he vanished into the red rock on which he was seated, or into the air itself, no one could say.

"The people looked up now, to where Thunderbird hovered, bloody but triumphant, in the air. Perhaps, they hoped, he could lift the awful curse. Perhaps he could restore this land as it had been. They would sacrifice to him again, and food would grow again in the land.

"But Thunderbird was silent. Tears for his people ran down his regal face, and the people knew that nothing could lift the curse. They knew that they would have to leave the desert and find their home even he could not make the desert bloom again.

"Silently and somberly they buried their dead, packed their belongings, made ready to begin their long trek, no one knew where, in search of fruitful land. The following morning they left, and wherever they went Thunderbird went with them. And they travelled for many years, and passed out of the sight of other men."

Jay Blueheels was somber. "It is an old story," he concluded. "For many years it was told around the Indians' fires. Recently it has not been heard very often. You are the first to hear it, Chong Fei K'ing, in many seasons. Each year now the Indian people keep its sad wisdom to themselves. And each year, at the harvest moon, they pray to Thunderbird, asking him to protect them for one more year, asking that this not be the year of the deadly harvest.

"It is a story you had to hear, young one. For tomorrow"— his gentle old face frowned—"we go to meet the Vulture."

CHAPTER NINE. *THIS SIDE OF HELL*

"Not even if it would save my life."

K'ing smiled in amused comprehension as the old Indian shook his head vehemently in rejection of his suggestion. It did not really surprise him that Jay Blueheels should be opposed to their using the Cadillac to save time in today's trek across the desert. But he had thought that in the circumstances, with less than a full day remaining before sunrise of the Equinox, he might make an exception to what the young Master realized was a deep-set distrust of the white man's machines.

Now he saw that that was impossible. Not only was the old man set in his ways, but, K'ing saw, he was standing on a point of principle. There was nothing that could budge him from his resolve to make the difficult journey by foot—not even the possibility of his death from over-exertion along the way. So it was more out of a sense of logical obligation than out of any real hope of success that he tried, feebly, to persuade the old man.

"Sometimes," he said, "it is necessary to take advantage of things that we do not like. If I had not used this automobile"—he pointed to the big Cadillac, gleaming like some abandoned icon in the shimmering morning sun—"I would not be here now. Is it so bad a thing to allow the white man's machinery to aid us now, when time is so short?"

Jay Blueheels met K'ing's inquisitive gaze evenly. "Young one," he said, "there are some things a man may not do and still call himself a man—no matter what the danger. The way to the place of the Vulture is long and hard. Many men have died trying to get there, and many more have died once they did arrive. If we put our bodies into this... collection of bolts... we would do dishonor to their memory. No. The way is by foot, and that is the only way."

"Even if it means that we do not reach the place in time?"

"It is two days' walk from here. When I was a young man I did the journey in one day. I can do the journey in one day again, and we have one day. We will go at the red man's pace: walk, then run, then walk again. Are you afraid that you will be unable to match the pace of an old man, young one?"

No, K'ing was not afraid. He smiled again as he saw that there was nothing more to be said on the point. He shrugged his resignation and bowed slightly. "Let us start, then."

117

K'ing chuckled as they passed the car, and clapped a hand down on the hood in mock farewell. They set out toward the sun.

Almost at once K'ing's fears that they would not reach the place in time were allayed. The old man was as hardy as the young Master himself, and K'ing knew that if it were humanly possible to cross the desert to their unknown rendezvous in the time left, he and the old Indian would be the ones to do it. K'ing watched the old man with growing respect as he labored with what seemed scant effort under the heat of a blazing sun. At once he was as efficient as the machine he despised: his leather-clad feet hit the hard-baked sand with a rhythm as regular as the seasons, his body moved easily, smoothly over the sand, the long arms loose at his sides, the lanky legs lapping up the miles as easily as if this wasteland were a natural habitat for a man. K'ing could see that, whatever his peculiarities, the old man was completely at home in the desert.

They had walked about ten minutes in silence when the old man turned to his companion and spoke softly.

"Now we run."

And they ran. The strain on their bodies of even this limited exertion was telling in the hundred degree heat of the valley, and yet K'ing saw that the old man showed no more than a slight heaviness in his breathing as evidence that the effort was punishing to him.

K'ing no longer thought of the car they had left behind. He saw now that the old man had been right, that this steady but grueling pace on foot was the only way. As his lungs began to ache with the pain, as the sweat began to course in small rivers down his face, his mind relaxed: there was a strange satisfaction in this kind of excessive physical labor, and the young Master's spirit welcomed the ordeal his body was now beginning, as the spirit of a fine athlete would welcome the start of a championship race.

They ran for ten minutes; then the old man slowed to a walk again. He turned to the boy beside him. Sweat covered his ruddy features, but his breath was not even labored.

"This is how it will go today, young one. Walk, then run, then walk again. There is not time enough to sleep, except maybe an hour or two this afternoon, when the sun is highest and even the scorpions hide from it. I can see you are a good runner, so we will make it in time. Do not worry."

K'ing's smile acknowledged and returned the compliment. "I was not worried," he said.

"Tomorrow," said the old man. "Tomorrow at noon we will reach the Devil's Hole. It is a good time and a bad time. Because tomorrow is the Night of the Crying Moon, and that means we have much to win, much to lose. Great deeds will be done. I am glad you have come."

K'ing mulled over the impact of the Indian's words as they set to a run again. Yes, there would be great deeds done, one way or another. His soul bristled with premature delight at the thought that in less than a day he would confront Kak Nan Tang.

And yet, he reflected, he was taking a great deal on faith. He had really no way of being sure that the old man was leading him to Kak, except that the simultaneity of the Vulture's coming feast day with the coming of Kak's Dark Harvest was simply too much to be taken as coincidence. He wondered what the connection was between the ancient death cult of the Indians and the Red Circle. And what was the connection between both of them and the mysterious millenarian group known as the Gathering?

In a sense none of this mattered, for he was certain that, at the end of this desert march, Kak would be waiting for him. He was as sure of it as he had ever been sure of anything in his life, and the certainty lent fire to his limbs and the freshness of cooling water to his burning lungs. He had an appointment with Kak, that much was certain. An appointment with the devil. That was all that mattered.

What was it the old man had called it? The Devil's Hole? A fitting name for their destination. K'ing wondered what it would look like, the site of their fateful rendezvous, but he decided to wait until they stopped for rest to discuss it with the old man.

The sun rose higher in the sky, and the desert was blank except for the two specks of black trudging defiantly across the sand. The sparse wildlife of the wasteland had decided, on this opening day of the harvest season, to spend the day indoors. As if summer were reluctant to leave, and were trying to make its last performance its best, the heat of the sun had never been more oppressive. The meteorologists in downtown Los Angeles, two hundred miles to the South, were at this moment sweating at their desks and marking up record highs on their weather charts. But here in Death Valley, the deepest and deadliest spot in the continental United States, no thermometers or barometers registered the

119

action of the sun. Only the gila monsters knew that this was a record heat, and they had long ago taken to their scrubbed-out retreats under rocks. They could not see the two madmen winding East into the eye of this impossible sun; they were drowsily oblivious to this single sign of life in death's domain.

Near two o'clock the old man stopped. He wiped the back of his hand across his forehead and smiled at K'ing. "We are a mile, maybe a mile and a half, ahead of time. Now we rest."

K'ing looked around him. Rest? Rest where? As far as his keen eyes sought, nothing but sagebrush, no more than a few inches high, interrupted the flatness of the landscape. His eyes squinted against the glare and he looked inquisitively at the old man.

Jay Blueheels smiled. "The gods did not think to supply the snakes with holes, and so the snakes have had to dig their own. We must do the same."

K'ing nodded and followed the Indian's lead. Soon they were on their knees side by side, their thin clothing stuck to their backs with moisture as they scooped handful after handful of dusty sand out to make a six foot round hole in the middle of the plain. They had dug about three feet down when K'ing became aware that the sand was less like powder, that it was taking on a more compact appearance and feel, almost as if it had been pressed together with moisture. They dug another foot and now he was almost certain that the sand was becoming moist. It certainly could not be called wet, but at least it did not simply sift through the young man's hands to the ground.

And it was not as hot either. Greedily K'ing tore at the desert floor, his whole aching body bent to the task. For now he was sure that the old man had a double reason for telling him to dig. One was to provide a hole that, the young Master knew, they could cover with their garments and so produce a kind of tent The other, he now dared to hope, was to unlock the moisture that always lay hidden deep beneath the sands of the most barren desert. He remembered how Lin Fong had been able to go for days and nights on end in the desert, and had never been known to take food or drink with him. Now he began to suspect that part of the "secret"—inwardly he chuckled at his Master's humorous admission, after his death, that there were in fact no secrets on this earth—of the old man's survival had been that, like the resourceful Indian digging at his side, he always knew where the gods had planted sustenance for the traveller. He scooped his hands again into the earth.

Until this moment K'ing had not realized how thirsty he was. Now, with the hope of drink only feet, perhaps inches, from his fingers, he dug with increased fervor. Beside him the old man kept up the same steady pace.

The hole was nearly six feet deep when K'ing felt the first patch of unmistakably moist earth on his fingers. With an almost smug grin he caught the Indian's eye. The man rubbed some brownish sand between his thumb and forefinger, and resumed digging. "All the comforts of home," K'ing heard him mutter.

In a half hour a small pool of muddy water had formed in the bottom of the hole. They were by this time seven or eight feet beneath the surface of the Valley, and already the hundred degree heat seemed to be abating. For what K'ing had learned the previous night about speed was equally true about temperature: when it was extremely high, the least increment or fall made a great deal of difference. It could not have been less than ninety-five at the bottom of the hole, and yet K'ing breathed as deeply and with as full a satisfaction as if he were inhaling Zhamballah's coolest breezes. It might be summer still at the surface, but here, seven feet closer to the earth's burning core, it was already fall.

Now the old man extended his hand and K'ing, reading his eyes without having to be told, handed him his shirt. Jay Blueheels took off his own shirt and K'ing was surprised at two things. One was how trim, how compact, the ancient flesh hung on his frame—a lifetime in the wilderness had certainly not made him soft. The other was the presence, just below the man's right shoulder, of a wicked-looking scar: a twisted, misshapen patch of skin that looked like the remains of a long and painful mutilation.

K'ing found himself staring at it, and hoped the indiscretion had not offended his guide. But the Indian said nothing. He only took the two garments and scampered up the sides of the small artificial cave. In a minute, with the aid of a few sage twigs, he had draped them over the opening, and the two travellers had their snake hole.

When he returned they drank, and K'ing was pleasantly surprised at how fresh the muddy water tasted. They closed their eyes, resting them for a moment against the midday sun, and then the old man spoke.

"You wonder about my scar." He touched the whitish, torn skin gingerly, as if it were not a disfigurement at all, but an old friend to be handled carefully. "This one, and this one"—he touched the twisted corner of his mouth—" were given to me a long time ago by one of the Vulture people. That should answer your other question too, which you are too polite to ask: why I am doing this. Did you not wonder about that before this, young one?"

K'ing shrugged. "I knew you must have your reasons. And I have mine. The rest I did not think important."

The old man returned his shrug. "Perhaps you are right, and perhaps not. Sometimes, though, it is good for men who travel together to know why they are travelling together. Not all pilgrims seek the same church."

"And yet they may walk together."

"That is true. But you should know that you and I, young one, do not fight the same fight. For today, and for tomorrow perhaps, we walk the same path. After that, who knows?"

K'ing was silent. It was clear to him that the old man who had been so far a faithful guide was burdened and wished to speak of something difficult. The young Master bowed slightly and raised an eyebrow. He said nothing.

"What you seek is the death of a man who has wronged you. And the destruction of Evil. That man's Evil. Perhaps all Evil. Evil in any form. It is not important how I know this. Let us say simply, to steal the words of an old acquaintance of both of us, that the Blue Circle is very wide."

K'ing's eyes went wide, then gradually softened, and the boy leaned back in the moist sand. He remembered how far Lin Fong had travelled, how many lands he had seen:

"My aims are less grand than yours," the old man continued. "Shorter, maybe smaller; but I do not think less important I too wish revenge. I too wish justice and the destruction of Evil. Yet the Evil of which I speak is not the Evil of the Red Circle or of the Red Circle's slaves. It is not that wide. You have taken the whole world for your battleground, I have concentrated on this Valley.

"And my aim is simple. That my people may regain what is rightfully theirs: the land which the white invaders have stolen from them. To gain that end I have led you this far, and tomorrow I will lead you still farther. For I am an old man, after all, and my body—strong as it may seem to you under this sun of my homeland—is not a fighting body. When the fighting begins tomorrow my body will be of no use to you or to myself.

"I have brought you here, you can see now, because your body is ripe for the fighting that mine is not. As to your soul, that I cannot judge. But I am not interested in that. What I need is your strength. What you need is my eyes. So we help each other. Now you know why I said what I did about pilgrims."

K'ing looked with a mixture of admiration and regret at the old man. Clearly this was a character of far greater complexities than any in the world of the white men he hated had ever given him credit for. There was no telling how long he had sat sequestered in this wasteland awaiting the day when someone with the speed and muscles he lacked would come to help him in his vengeance against the murderers of his people.

The young Master heard his announcement calmly, but d-d not know how to respond. Surely the old man understood that the fate of a few people here in the vast American wasteland was of relatively little importance when weighed against the suffering that the Red Circle could inflict against millions of people around the world if Kak were left unchecked? Surely the Vulture people were almost incidental here—it was Kak, who had captured the minds of that fanatic sect and turned it to his own devices, who was the central villain?

And yet K'ing saw also that, at a deeper level, it was all the same fight. That the suffering inflicted on the Indian people here in California by the white man was in its own way the same thing as the suffering inflicted by Kak on any of a million innocents he had attacked in the past, and might attack in the future.

Perhaps the old man was right. Evil was Evil, no matter who was doing the acting. Was it not the duty of the follower of the Tao to meet and combat Evil in whatever form it took?

Again the young Master felt the burden of a dilemma with which Lin Fong had presented him years before. One must not do Evil. And one can never be certain what is Evil and what is not. And yet one must not do Evil. Was the old Indian before him, his eyes a wash of curiosity, mild amusement, and a kind of tortured sympathy, saying to him that, in some as yet indefinable way, what K'ing was about to do was, in its own manner, Evil as well? The thought grieved him; he shook his head as if to clear it of an unaccustomed and, in the circumstances, unhealthy cynicism; and responded with as much respect as he knew the old man deserved.

"For the moment we fight the same fight, old one. Is that not enough for you?"

"Today it is enough. Tomorrow perhaps it will be enough. The next day—who knows? I have had many friends in my day, young one. Some of them are still friends, and many have gone away. You and I? We may yet walk away from each other. I do not know."

Suddenly the old man's face broke out into a radiant smile, as if to dispel the clouds that his words had suggested to K'ing's mind. "It is only something to think about, young one. But now you must not think. Now you must rest. In two hours we begin again."

K'ing bowed again and closed his eyes. The disturbing thoughts did not leave his mind, but his body was, at least momentarily, exhausted from the desert trek, and allowed him to sleep. Across from him his guide closed his eyes too.

When K'ing awoke he was aware of a third presence in the shaded hole. His eyes came up fast and met those of the old man, who spoke from between tightened lips. "Look slowly to your left. There, in the water. Do not move."

K'ing's eyes drifted left. From the muddy water protruded the triangular head of a desert rattler. It was quiet. There was no sign yet of the bony clatter that signified the snake was about to strike.

"He comes in out of the sun. It is a good sign. If we can kill him we will eat well. Then we can begin again."

The old man smiled across the small pool at the boy. Two feet from K'ing's leg the rattler rearranged its coils in the cooling water. The old man spoke again.

"He is a gift of the desert. Good luck."

K'ing smiled back his thanks. It was evident that the old man could not get at the deadly snake without first rising and shifting his position to be close enough to strike out with his knife. And that would alert the nervous reptile, cause him to attack. The snake was quite near to K'ing, however, and so it was up to him.

The rattler moved and K'ing prepared to strike. Something in the tensing of the boy's muscles had tipped the snake off: now it was ready, sensing danger, sensing attack. In a second it would whip out at the nearest moving object, and at the moment that was K'ing's ankle.

The triangle rose from the water and began to sway. K'ing braced himself against the wall of the hole and breathed thinly through his nose. Inches from his foot the rattler wavered.

Then the whirring began. K'ing let it go a second, two seconds, three. His left hand straightened, became stiff. His mind relaxed and told him the path the striking head would take.

Suddenly the rattle stopped.

K'ing's hand was the tail of a deadly scorpion. It met the snapping form just behind the head, and the young Master's fist closed brutally on the writhing form before the snake could twist the deadly fangs toward his wrist. For a second he displayed the catch to his companion. Then the powerful fingers closed slowly and breath left the reptile's body and he lay limp in the young Master's hand. K'ing grabbed the body by the tail and handed it to his host.

They clambered out of the hole. Jay Blueheels took flint and steel from his pocket and went in search of sagebrush. In a few minutes he returned, and the desert air was filled with the smell of roasting meat.

They ate, and set out again.

For the next few hours they travelled in silence. The heat grew gradually less oppressive as the day wore on, and by sundown K'ing had fully accustomed himself to the grueling walk-run-walk pace set by his aged companion.

At nightfall Jay Blueheels called another halt, and the two travellers sat around a small campfire for another two hours, surrounded by endless miles of flat sand and the occasional cry of an owl or a coyote. Then they were off again toward the East.

Travelling at night, K'ing found, was far easier than travelling by day. The worst of the desert heat had gone by sundown, and now all he had to contend with was the growing fatigue of his body. He marvelled at the old man's apparently unlimited reservoirs of strength, and, as so many times before in his short but active, life, he committed his mind to the Tao, from which, he trusted now as ever, all endurance flowed.

It was less than two hours till dawn when Jay Blueheels called a final halt.

"Rest now," the old man said. "When you wake we will have but one more leg of our journey. Out there"—he pointed to the East, which was now still a black horizon—"lies the Devil's Hole. You will see it when you awaken. It is the tallest of several large rock peaks that dot the horizon North to South. From where we now sit, the sun appears to rise exactly behind it, and watching the sun when you awake will tell you which rock to make for. I tell you this now because there is no telling what the morning sun will bring, and I may not be able to show you these things tomorrow. Sleep now."

And K'ing slept.

CHAPTER TEN. *AND THE BLIND SHALL SEE*

He awoke to the sound of screeching.

The young Master opened his eyes quickly and turned his eyes to the East where, he remembered, Jay Blueheels had told him his journey this morning would end.

The first thing he saw was the Devil's Hole. A huge crag of red rock, it towered above the horizon in cruel majesty less than a mile from where he sat.

Then, half way between him and the rock, K'ing saw something else. It was a fight, and it was from there that the screeching sound had come. He narrowed his eyes against the sun and tried to focus through the haze.

It was two figures.

A man. And a gigantic bird.

Jay Blueheels and a great bird of prey. The old Indian was waving his arms and covering his head against the repeated attacks of the bird, and K'ing could see he was in trouble. In a single smooth motion the young Master was on his feet and off streaking toward the fight.

The racing form of the Master caught the eye of the deadly predator and it turned its head to face the new intruder. Its giant wings still beating the air about the old man's head, it swiped at his eyes one last time and then set its attention to K'ing.

The young Master's arms went up in a sweeping defensive gesture just as the bird wheeled toward him, his talons grasping the air. K'ing's fist came up hard and the bird staggered back, marking time in the air, waiting for an opening against this strange new opponent. The desert dweller was used to death. He was not so accustomed to life. He had never before seen such grace, such limitless energy, in any of the creatures of his domain. The small spinning figure would be no easy prey for him. He came down cautiously.

When the deadly talons struck at his face, K'ing's head bobbed down and left. His hands came up again in a blinding flurry of savage slashes. The bird wheeled back. Not even the snakes, whose delectable meat had been worth the tremendous fight they put up, had ever given him this much trouble. Even with the immense advantage of his great maneuverability, he could not find an opening through the dodging figure's arms.

For ten minutes they fenced. Feathers and blood flew into the air. The bird swooped down again and again, but each time the flashing hands of the young Master fended him off. Eventually the bird tired of the fruitless fight. He saw there would be no killing here—no food for him and his hungry brood. The man creature who blocked his every advance would not be killed. He would have to hunt elsewhere. With a last shuddering screech he wheeled off toward the sun, as if by exhibiting the magnificence of his flight he could forget the indignity of his defeat.

For a second K'ing watched the giant shape drift into the eye of the sun. Then he turned his attention to his wounded comrade.

Jay Blueheels would live, but he had been badly battered. Blood covered his face, and about the eyes deep gouges ran richly red. His thin tunic was in shreds. Deep scratches ran the length of his arms, and his chest had been scarred by what looked like a vicious lashing.

But the old man was not beaten yet, and K'ing smiled grimly to see the attempt he was making to speak. His thin lips parted in a series of quick jerks, and the voice was hoarse but strong.

"It is time, young one," he said. "Look to the sun. In another two hours it will be your time."

K'ing shielded his eyes against the desert glare. The bird was far up by now, a dot against the sun. In a couple of hours, he figured, it would be noon. He looked back to the old man.

"Lie still and do not speak. I will get you water."

For the second time in two days K'ing thrust his hands into the blazing sand of Death Valley. He dug as if possessed, and beside him the battered form of his companion and guide made no sound. In five minutes he had scooped out a hole three feet deep. Another three and he would feel the moisture again. He pulled at the sand as if trying to rip out the very heart of the desert itself, and in another ten minutes his labor was rewarded.

He scampered out of the pit and went to the old man. The Indian was breathing heavily, and K'ing knew that if he did not get him help, or at least shade, soon, he might the here within sight of the Devil's Hole. Gingerly, with a grave reverence, he lifted the sagging body in his arms and carried it to the hole. Cradling the old man so the jostling would not shake more blood out of his already

128

desiccated and badly bled frame, he slid down the steep side of the pit into the small pool of water at the bottom.

The old man's eyes thanked him and then closed as K'ing brought cupped hands to his lips. Jay Blue-heels drank slowly, then laid his head back in the sand. "I will rest now," he said.

K'ing tore a corner of the old man's shirt off and wet it in the muddy pool. He applied the cloth tenderly to his many wounds, watching the red run down his neck and onto the flat, surprisingly muscular chest. His body was a mass of scratches and lacerations, but Jay Blueheels would live. K'ing could see that. It would take more than a chance attack by a desert demon to kill off this hardy creature.

The old man had been resting fitfully for about an hour when a huge white spotlight appeared through the cloth that K'ing had stretched over the top of the hole as an awning. Immediately the Indian's eyes snapped awake, and K'ing, who had been watching his charge with a mixture of admiration and concern, looked up too.

The sun was almost at the zenith. "It is time," said Jay Blueheels.

K'ing's handsome features closed into a mild frown. "You must rest, old man. Rest, and then we will go on."

"No," replied the Indian. "You must go on. Now. I cannot travel now, but I will travel soon again." He looked about the artificial cave that his young companion had constructed for him. "You have learned the ways of the desert well. You have made me a good home here, and it is all that I need. Nothing can harm me here. So it is time for you to go."

K'ing thought of the snake that he had killed the day before. If one of its brothers should fall into the hole, would the old man have the strength to kill it? Would he have the strength to climb out of this temporary retreat and make his way back to Jimson Flats? And what if K'ing himself were killed in the coming fight? What would the old man do then, alone and unprotected in this vast wasteland?

"No. I cannot leave you yet. There is time yet."

The Indian's face hardened into a frown. "Young one," he said firmly, "remember what I have said about pilgrims. A time comes for a man to take his own way. To leave his companions. It is a difficult thing to do, but a man must do many difficult things.

Go now. Climb up and look to the East. You will see that what I say is true. You will see that it is time for you to go."

K'ing hesitated and the old man spoke once again. "A man must follow his own way."

The Son of the Flying Tiger rose slowly and turned his face toward the noonday sun. Well, he thought, if it will make the old man happy I will leave this hole for a minute. I will not leave him as he demands. But I will go up for a minute, until he falls asleep again, and then I will watch over him from there.

With a light wave of farewell K'ing scrambled again up the side of the pit. His eyes squinted instinctively against the unbearable brightness of the sun. Then he looked to the Devil's Hole.

What he saw made him blink and look again..

The old man had been right.

His time was come.

Standing defiantly against the red of the rock was a black-clad figure about his own height. The clothes fit tightly and the figure stood with an easy grace against the ruggedness of the landscape. His hands on his hips, he leaned nonchalantly away from the wall of rock behind him, and seemed to stretch out mockingly across the small space between them. His black unruly hair blew lightly in the desert wind.

K'ing did not have to look closely to see who it was. As soon as he had climbed out of the hole, some precise hidden sense had let him know that his arch enemy was not far away. The sight of Kak Nan Tang before the Devil's Hole only confirmed what his instincts already knew.

For a few seconds the two Kung Fu Masters stared at each other across the glaring white of the desert. Then, slowly, almost ceremonially, the figure before the rock raised its arms in a kind of salute, and K'ing heard a single word ring mockingly from the distant throat.

It was the word he most feared. Now it came to him with all the brutal transparency of his vision in the mirror.

"Brother!"

Kak might just as well have placed a burning poker on his naked body. Instantly all thought of the old man in the hole behind him was forgotten, and his weary body surged anew with energy for the fight.

He charged.

The figure stood calmly, not moving a muscle.

Then, when K'ing was only twenty yards from him, and he could see the two purplish scars clearly, Kak disappeared.

For a haunting awful second K'ing felt that Black Magic had somehow transported his enemy to another realm. Immediately his coolly rational mind dismissed the notion as nonsense, and he realized what had actually happened.

Kak had gone into the rock. Into the Devil's Hole!

K'ing came up hard against the steaming red outcropping and searched for an opening. It took him only a second to locate the narrow crevice and at once he slipped his body through.

It was noon of the Equinox, and the Master of the Earthly Center had entered the Devil's Hole.

His keen eyes immediately ranged through the dim light, picked up the circle, the occult symbols, the shallow dome. Kak was nowhere to be seen. K'ing might have been in a tomb from which all spirits had fled.

Then, as the sun reached the zenith, light poured into the cavern. From high above his head K'ing could see the narrow shaft of pure sunlight lancing through the air in a perfectly straight line to illuminate a spot exactly between his feet. K'ing looked up at the brilliant pinpoint, and suddenly he found himself rooted to the spot. He tried to move but could not. He was as immobile, as incapable of the least exertion, as he had been when his eyes had fallen on the strange talon for the first time at the New Age commune.

And he could not keep his eyes off the light Mystified and disturbed, K'ing glared back at the tiny window to the sun, attempting to break the spell, but he could do nothing. Whatever magic Kak had developed in this secluded spot, it was at this single unholy moment powerful enough to bring even the exquisitely tuned senses of the Blue Circle Master to a standstill. K'ing had never felt so helpless in his life.

He did not know how long the light kept him captive. But suddenly, it was gone, and the cavern was pitch black again. K'ing raised his hand to his head, tried to concentrate on the wisdom of Zhamballah, shook his head angrily. He could see nothing. It was as if he had stared for hours into the piercing desert sun, and his sight had left him for good. He groped in the darkness trying to ascertain where he had come in, where Kak might have gone out.

And then he heard it.

131

Behind him. Maybe three, maybe four feet off to the left.

A low gutteral sound, a snatch in the throat, a deliberate mockery of a death rattle.

The sound was not that of a rattler. It came from no earthly throat. It came from the throat of the boy who had pledged his earthly existence to the service of the agents of Evil. It was a signal and a greeting from the single being on the earth for whom K'ing had allowed himself to feel hatred.

In utter darkness K'ing whirled on his heel to face the unseen presence. In darkness they would meet and in darkness they would fight. For he knew that somewhere in this tiny rock enclosure, no more than feet from him, was the grinning, mocking face of Kak Nan Tang.

He listened.

No sound disturbed the tomblike silence of the cave. He wondered if it really were a cave, or if by some quirk of chance or necromancy he had been transported, at the height of the Equinox, to some dark realm where physical laws were suspended and the malicious designs of Zedak ruled the universe. He wondered whether Kak could see in this hole, or whether the mystic powers he had been developing through the last few months of their separation had prepared him to see in the dark. Was he to fight a man or a fiend?

K'ing put these thoughts from his mind. Kak was a man and he was a man. And a man could fight. A man could use the serene beauty of Kung Fu, even in the dark of the grave. He bent his right ear slightly forward and listened.

For several minutes nothing happened as the two perfectly matched Masters—one the champion of the Way, the other the architect of Pain—faced each other unseen in the narrow confines of the Hole.

Then K'ing's ears caught the slightest scrape of shoe leather against stone. It was about four feet in front and to the left. Rapidly his mind calculated where that would place his opponent. Where if the sound-came from the left foot, and where if it came from the right. No, it would have to be from the right, for the gutteral sound had come from directly behind him, and he had turned in a perfect semicircle. So Kak would be facing him directly, four feet away.

Neither Master breathed. The silence was as total as if the cave held no living form.

K'ing waited, calculated again.

And then he struck.

Had Kak's head been in the exact spot K'ing had determined it would be he would have been dead, A vicious Tiger Claw would have torn out his eyes. But the evil Master had sensed the attack even before it began, and his head had moved quickly to the left as the hand darted out. K'ing's fingers scraped painfully down the hard walls of the cavern, and his ears took in the scraping of his enemy's shoes as he dodged.

Good, he thought. He had missed, but now he was sure his enemy was here. And he knew where he was.

K'ing went into a low crouch and came up flashing a double Knife Point where he knew Kak's solar plexus would be. He was met by the crushingly powerful force of a Boulder Block, and he backed off instantly to regauge his position. That instant reaction saved his life, for Kak had followed up the block with a withering Pounding Wave that passed so close to the young Master's face that the rush of wind felt cool on his face.

K'ing was not thinking now. Not with his mind. Some deep inward sense of proportion and space was thinking for him, and it was sending his arm out again in a savage Knife Slash before Kak could withdraw the arm K'ing knew was now directly in front of him. He cut down with the fury of suppressed rage.

But the same sense that was serving K'ing was also serving his adversary, and K'ing's fingers caught only the edge of a wrist bone as his opponent swept the arm back.

Back, and then forward again. K'ing felt the Hammer Blow coming before it was half way to his face, and his head was three inches to the right before it got there. He circled a few inches in that direction and sent a Lightning Kick three feet off the ground. He felt his foot connect with muscle and then felt Kak twist sharply to his own right, bending and softening the blow.

K'ing had the feel of this kind of fighting now. It was only a matter of judging where your opponent would be, and then striking there with conviction.

His position could be judged by the sound of heels on the floor, by the swift intakes of breath which said he was about to deliver a blow, by the very feel of his bones and muscles when you touched them.

133

Had Kak been an ordinary opponent, K'ing knew, he could have killed him long ago. He saw now that his Kung Fu practices and meditations had given him not only complete control over his body, but also an exceptionally fine sense of his surroundings, and their relation to his body. That meant that he could easily have defeated a less expert fighter in these circumstances, even if the other fighter could see. K'ing did not have to see. His body made moves blindly, and those moves, he was absolutely convinced, would never be wrong as long as he remained alert to the information which his other four senses—and that curious sixth sense that all great Masters knew was the secret of perfection—gave to him.

But Kak was no ordinary opponent. K'ing had just connected with a Lightning Kick, that was true, but Kak had come very close in the last minute to killing him twice, and that meant that he was, whether or not he had had any practice at it, as adept at this kind of combat as K'ing was himself. K'ing could take nothing for granted here.

They circled a moment, feeling out the space between them. Then, one of the powerful bodies moved forward, a stone shifted, and the two exploded into action again.

This time it was Kak who attacked first. His Elephant Kick rushed out to pin his enemy to the wall, and K'ing grimaced in pain as the heavy foot glanced off his hip and he swerved to the right. He responded with a Dragon Stamp, and Kak met it first with a Monkey Blow that barely missed shattering the kneecap, then with a Knife Point aimed where he knew K'ing's throat would be.

But the young Master's throat was not there. That indefinable something in the tension of his opponent's body, that slight shift of heaviness in the air, had warned him in time. He whirled out of the way and chopped at Kak's arm with a right-handed Hammer Blow while his left became a Ram's Head aimed at Kak's crotch.

Kak's defense would have been brilliant even for a man who could see. Here in the utter darkness of the cave it was nothing less than superb. His left arm caught the descending Hammer and flung it backwards in a powerful Leaping Deer Block, while the right protected his threatened middle with a smooth, descending Whipping Branch. Then his foot came up fast at K'ing's exposed genitals.

The young Master flung himself back to the far wall and the foot that was meant to crush his testicles to paste whipped up toward the blackened dome.

That put the Red Circle Master off balance, and K'ing wasted no time in taking advantage of it. Rebounding off the wall with deadly speed he came back at Kak's head, his heels extended, searching...

But Kak too fell back, and K'ing was forced to scramble to his feet and out of the way of a searing volley of Ram's Heads. He retreated and leaned against the wall, not breathing.

But he had no time to rest. Kak's superb internal radar had tracked him almost immediately, and now the young Master ducked violently beneath the flying heels of his adversary. One of them caught him on the top of the head, and he shook it, stunned as Kak backed off for another attack.

When it came the young Master was no longer there. Kak's foot pounded into the rock of the wall, and K'ing homed in on the sound even before the deadly steel-tipped shoes had left the stone. His Scorpion Blow came down with a sharp crack on bone, and K'ing knew that he had cracked the unseen ankle.

It was a serious injury. With only one good leg Kak would not be able to fling himself far in the leaping attacks of which his theatrical mind was so fond. K'ing waited again, his ears and his very skin alive to the motions in the tiny room.

Yes, he could hear Kak breathing hard now, and he knew mat the broken ankle was troubling him. He crouched again, to invite the lower kicks that he knew his enemy would now have to use, and placed his hands loosely before him. When the kick came he grabbed the good ankle with the same precise, savage speed with which he had pinioned the snake the day before, and put all the force of his powerful grip into breaking it.

But Kak twisted away with a dull screech of surprise and pain. Perhaps he had forgotten that, no matter what advantage he had in this dark hole in which he was relatively at home, the young man he had challenged was no ordinary opponent. He came back again, breathing heavily now, rage in his throat, the rage that K'ing knew was both Kak's most terrifying attribute—and the single element mat could be his undoing. When a fighter began to show emotion he was done for. K'ing knew this perhaps better than his otherwise perfectly matched opponent, and it was that knowledge that had given him the edge in this dungeon.

He felt the crippled form hobbling toward him and struck. Above the ankles, though, Kak's defenses were as good as ever, and K'ing had nothing to show for his Knife-Slash Blow but the bruised wrist that Kak's expert Swooping Bird had made on it.

Then, suddenly, there was silence. K'ing knew something was wrong. He sensed that his enemy knew he was almost beaten, and would not be staying for the finish. The cave seemed empty again. No sound disturbed the stillness.

And yet K'ing still sensed the presence of his archenemy. He waited. His ears strained to pick up the fall of a pebble, the rise of breath, anything... And the rattle came again.

This time it came from the side. As if it were indeed the rattle of a deadly snake, K'ing immediately jumped to his left out of the way of the darting triangle. Again he was directly across the circle from the sound.

And it stopped.

K'ing got ready to spring. His legs tightened, his arms swayed, his hands began to form the dreaded Tiger Claw.

But then a second sound came up in the stillness of the cave, and this sound stopped him in stiff, dumb awareness. He had heard this sound before. Again he felt himself unable to move, and he was forced to listen to the words he most hated to hear.

It was the sound of a thousand rushing rivers. The sound of dust in the desert and dust in the plains and dust like a cloud of locusts over all the green places of the earth. The sound of his undoing, and of the mirror of his fate. It swept around him and he squirmed as if he were being burned as, from out of the deafening noise, the familiar voice of his archenemy mouthed again the terrifying word:

"Brother!"

And the blackness began to lift. K'ing stared, fascinated and disgusted, at the far wall. Slowly it brightened, shimmered, shone. It became a mirror. The mirror of his dream. And in the mirror glared the cruelly scarred face of Kak Nan Tang.

But whatever power had enabled Kak to lure the Blue Circle Master into the Hole at just this hour, was a power that did not play favorites. Now it served K'ing as well as it had served his enemy.

And K'ing knew. From somewhere beyond the knowing of men and the knowing even of the mystical circles of which the two were a part, he instantly understood the meaning of this vision. He knew what Kak had been trying to do to him all these weeks, and he knew that now, having once seen that cruel face turn into his own, he could not again be fooled. Kak had tricked him, but he would not trick him again. The man who had called him Brother would never seduce him again. From deep within the strength of his terror, from wells of courage and human understanding deeper even than the wells of Zhamballah, K'ing looked straight into the black eyes of the vision.

And laughed.

His laughter broke the mirror. It crumbled in a thousand pieces at his feet, and once again, in darkness, he faced the crippled, branded form of Kak Nan Tang.

Like a cat to the death, he leaped.

And the wall rushed up to meet him, and he hit it with a sound that opened his ears to hear and that drowned out, for a last time in this bizarre Valley, the sound of the river of death.

Kak was gone, and the body of the young Master crumbled to the cavern floor.

But his spirit sang on the wind.

EPILOGUE

"Welcome to the land of the living, kid."

K'ing was conscious. He opened his eyes slowly, saw white. He looked around the hospital room and into the grave but pleased face of Joe Corcoran. He was dimly aware that his body was in some pain, but right now he was glad to be in the world of clean sheets and wall clocks, and it took no great effort to pay attention to the words of the husky police lieutenant. He nodded his recognition and his mouth opened.

"How did I get here?"

"Now, don't you do no talking now. The doc says you're going to be fit as rain in a few days, but you been through some hard times and he don't want you to put no strain on yourself just yet. It's a lucky thing that crazy old Indian got to us when he did, or you'd still be lying in that goddamn cave close to dead. When we got there you looked like you been hit by a wall, and there was this gas coming out of the walls real slow. Another few hours and you'd of been a goner."

K'ing labored to speak again. "The Indian brought me here? How is he?"

"Shit, you can't kill no Indian that easy. He's fine. Back out in the desert I suppose. Sends his regards, though."

Joe lit a cigarette and inhaled deeply. He saw he had the young Master's attention, and he smiled with uncustomary warmth.

"You know, kid, they had more shit out in that place than Mrs. O'Leary's cow had flies. Mirrors, pulleys, sliding panels, weird recordings, light shows, smoke bombs, you name it. Spence says he ain't seen anything like it in five years. Whoever was running the operation sure knew what he was doing. Looked like a goddamn school for weirdoes. You ought to see the bastards we rounded up, too. Every big time weirdo from here to San Francisco. The stripper chick, she was just one out of about twenty. It looks like your buddy Kak—or whoever it was—was trying to get all the Satanist and occult groups in the area together under one flag, then put the whammy on the straight world but good. Almost did it too, and would of if you hadn't of been there to cramp his style.

"Too bad about the girl. When we broke into the cavern underground—there was this huge cave underground, you see, that you got to by a secret passage in that Devil's Hole—we found her flat on her back, nude, in the center of some sort of ancient temple. The profs over at UCLA are pretty damn excited about it—think it's the remains of some lost civilization, you know.

"Anyway, the girl had been given so much goddamn smack that she was bloated up like a balloon. That ain't a pretty way to go, I'll tell you."

K'ing closed his eyes in grim recognition. He knew where the ways of the Vulture ended and those of the Red Circle began. Then he opened his eyes again and nodded to Joe to continue.

"Well, there ain't much more to tell, actually. Spence figures the case is as good as closed now. Figures that whoever was behind it was trying to make as much trouble as possible by building up tension in the ranks of the weirdo sects here, and then take over the whole act himself. So he bumps off the Blake guy and dumps it on the commune doorstep to make it look like war between them. He decks these saps out in black tights and manages to convince them they're tight with some real big-time freak called the Vulture, and they go slashing folks' eyes out. He kidnaps every occult heavy in the area and either brainwashes them or drugs them until they're all working for him. He had big plans all right. This dark harvest crap was no joke. Looks like he was out to kill off a lot more folks before he was done. We found a list of potential allies, you know, to join the weirdoes he already had. Must have about forty, fifty names on it. We're working on that now. It's a good thing you got there when you did.

"Well, anyway, I just came in to see how you were. I'll be getting back now."

Joe rose to go, but K'ing spoke once more. "Was there any sign of Kak?".

"Your weird buddy with the scars? Yeah, well, Spence figures you were right about him. The freaks we rounded up, none of them is taking credit for any of the murders. Naturally. But we were careful to keep them isolated, to check their stories against each other. They're pretty consistent in describing the leader, and it looks like he fits your description of Kak. Don't you worry about him, though. There's enough fingerprints around that rock to put him away for good when we get him."

K'ing smiled grimly as the husky policeman waved a friendly farewell and went out the door. He wished it were that simple.

When Joe returned to the station house he assured his partner that the young Master would be up and around in a few days, and confirmed that the hospital had notified his next of kin in New York. Then he walked to his desk and looked again at the list of potential Red Circle converts which had been taken from the hideout under the Devil's Hole. Of the thirty-odd names on the list, about half had been crossed off as either dead or already in jail. The rest were still to be considered suspects. Next to many of these names Spencer had placed a question mark, indicating that the police as yet had no record of them. These would be the hardest to locate, and probably would be untraceable. They would just have to hope that the real heavies were the ones who already had records.

"Any more luck on the list?" Spencer's voice was a little weary, overwrought with the passing of tension that always hit him when a case ended.

Joe scanned the list again. Half way down it, beside one of the question marks, appeared the name "Oswald, Lee Harvey." In this balmy late summer of 1963, almost two months before the assassin's bullet would end the life of the youngest President in the country's history, the name struck no bell. "Nothing," he said.

"May as well file it, then," said Spencer. "We got other things to do."